Welcome to the new ~~collection~~ of Harlequin Presents!

Don't miss contributions from favorite authors Michelle Reid, Kim Lawrence and Susan Napier, as well as the second part of Jane Porter's THE DESERT KINGS series, Lucy Gordon's passionate Italian, Chantelle Shaw's Tuscan tycoon and Jennie Lucas's sexy Spaniard! And look out for Trish Wylie's brilliant debut Presents book, *Her Bedroom Surrender!*

We'd love to hear what you think about Harlequin Presents. E-mail us at Presents@hmb.co.uk or join in the discussions at www.iheartpresents.com and www.sensationalromance.blogspot.com, where you'll also find more information about books and authors!

Harlequin Presents®

ITALIAN HUSBANDS

They're tall, dark…and ready to marry!

If you love reading about our sensual Italian men, don't delay, look out for the next story in this great miniseries!

Kim Lawrence

SECRET BABY, CONVENIENT WIFE

ITALIAN HUSBANDS

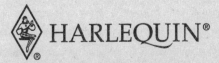

HARLEQUIN®

TORONTO • NEW YORK • LONDON
AMSTERDAM • PARIS • SYDNEY • HAMBURG
STOCKHOLM • ATHENS • TOKYO • MILAN • MADRID
PRAGUE • WARSAW • BUDAPEST • AUCKLAND

ISBN-13: 978-0-373-12724-5
ISBN-10:   0-373-12724-3

SECRET BABY, CONVENIENT WIFE

First North American Publication 2008.

Copyright © 2008 by Kim Lawrence.

All about the author...
Kim Lawrence

Though lacking much authentic Welsh blood,
KIM LAWRENCE—from English/Irish stock—
was born and brought up in north Wales. She
returned there when she married, and her sons
were both born on Anglesey, an island off the
coast. Though not isolated, Anglesey is a little off
the beaten track, but lively Dublin, which Kim
loves, is only a short ferry ride away.

Today they live on the farm her husband was
brought up on. Welsh is the first language of
many people in this area and Kim's husband and
sons are all bilingual. She is having a lot of fun,
not to mention a few headaches, trying to learn
the language!

With small children, she thought the unsocial
hours of nursing weren't too attractive, so,
encouraged by a husband who thinks she
can do anything she sets her mind to, Kim tried
her hand at writing. Always a keen Harlequin
reader, she felt it was natural for her to write a
romance novel. Now she can't imagine doing
anything else.

She is a keen gardener and cook, and enjoys
running—often on the beach because, living
on an island, the sea is never very far away. She
is usually accompanied by her Jack Russell,
Sprout—don't ask, it's a long story!

CHAPTER ONE

DERVLA'S skirt lifted in the updraft as the helicopter carrying their guests lifted off. Her husband—it had taken her three months before she could use the term even in the privacy of her own thoughts—laughed huskily, his dark eyes glinting with amusement as he watched her frenzied efforts to smooth the fabric back down modestly over her thighs.

She gave him a half-hearted glare, avoiding prolonged exposure to those mocking eyes because mingled in with the amusement was a glint of insolent sexual challenge that made her hand shake slightly as she lifted it to smooth her tousled red hair into a semblance of order—never an easy objective to achieve where her wayward pre-Raphaelite curls were concerned.

Gianfranco made no attempt to restore order to his own mussed dark hair, but he looked gorgeous anyway.

With his glorious vibrant Mediterranean colouring, dark fallen-angel features and six-foot-five lean, muscle-packed frame, Gianfranco Bruni could not not look gorgeous if he tried!

Gorgeous in a way that triggered a hot hormonal rush and made the muscles low in Dervla's pelvis tighten when she looked at him; gorgeous in a way that never failed to make her throat tighten with emotion she had no trouble putting a name to—but she didn't!

While not mentioning love had not been included in their

marriage vows, it might as well have been because Gianfranco had made his own feelings on the subject crystal-clear when he had proposed.

He had proposed!

Now how bizarre was that?

Gianfranco arched a darkly delineated brow and looked down at her, one corner of his wide sensual mouth lifting in a teasing half-smile. 'What does that enigmatic little smile mean, *cara mia*?'

Dervla shivered as he traced the curve of her mouth with the pad of one long brown finger and tilted her face up to his like a flower seeking sunlight. She turned her flushed cheek into the curve of his hand as she looked at him through her lashes, marvelling at the perfect symmetry of his slashing cheekbones, velvety dark eyes and sensually sculpted lips.

'I just have to pinch myself sometimes. It all seems so surreal.'

His darkly delineated brows drew together above his aquiline nose. 'And bruise such perfect flawless skin?' he said, allowing his finger to drop, trailing sensuously down over the pale flesh of her neck until it came to rest in the pulse spot at the base of her throat.

Dervla swallowed as the slumberous heat in his dark eyes made her wildly sensitive stomach flip and her heartbeat stumble and quicken.

'I can't think straight when you look at me like that and we still have a guest, Gianfranco,' she protested, her heart skipping another beat as his wicked smile flashed, deepening the sexy creases around his bold dark eyes.

'Carla?' Frowning at the reminder, he dismissed his distant cousin with an eloquent shrug of one shoulder. 'I don't know why you invited her anyway. It was meant to be a weekend to catch up with Angelo and Kate.'

The gentle reproach made Dervla's green eyes widen in incredulity.

'Me invite her?' Not only had Gianfranco issued the invitation to the gorgeous brunette, but he'd forgotten to even mention it to her!

So when the older woman had appeared looking her usual immaculately groomed self with an amount of luggage that had seemed to Dervla more appropriate to a two-month luxury cruise than an informal weekend in the country, Dervla had had to think on her feet and pretend she knew all about it.

And Gianfranco himself had not exactly helped the situation when, on heaving himself dripping from the pool, he had found the older woman watching him through her designer shades.

His, 'What are you doing here, Carla?' had not exactly oozed warmth and welcome!

Actually he'd said it in Italian, but Dervla's command of the language had progressed to the point where she could even get the gist of fairly rapid conversations. She despaired of her accent, but Gianfranco had promised her it was extremely sexy.

Dervla didn't entirely believe him, but it was always flattering to be told you were sexy, especially by a man who was lusted after by every female under ninety that came in contact with him!

'I know you two are friendly, but I would like my wife to myself sometimes.'

Friendly?

Dervla felt a spasm of guilt. She ought to think of Gianfranco's cousin as a friend; the other woman had gone out of her way to make Dervla feel at home when she had arrived.

If it hadn't been for Carla's tactful suggestions she could have made a number of painful faux pas—actually she'd made them anyway, but that was because she didn't always accept the older woman's very good advice.

It had been Carla who had supplied the identity of the gorgeous, nubile young woman who had plastered herself against Gianfranco as they did a circuit of the dance floor when everyone else she had asked changed the subject or pleaded ignorance.

Carla had explained about the blonde's on/off relationship with Gianfranco. It seemed that they picked up the threads of their relationship when it suited them both.

'More of a habit than a relationship, really,' she observed dismissively.

Habits, Dervla thought, watching Gianfranco's ex-girlfriend trail her scarlet fingertips down his lapel before drawing his face down to kiss his lips, were hard to break.

Even if you wanted to, and she wasn't sure in the early days Gianfranco did!

Carla advised her not to bring up the subject.

'You really mustn't feel insecure about it, Dervla, because I'm sure he would never disrespect you by being unfaithful.'

Carla was the only one who didn't clam up when she mentioned Sara, Gianfranco's first wife and mother of his son.

'He adored her,' Carla confided when she walked into a room and saw Dervla staring at a framed portrait by a famous photographer of a newborn Alberto in the arms of his mother, who had the serene look of a glowing Madonna.

Not exactly news, but it had made Dervla's spirits sink like a lead weight anyway.

If she considered anyone a friend here in Italy it really ought to be Carla. Yet somehow she never felt totally easy in the Italian woman's sophisticated company.

Maybe, she mused, it was because of the incident just after her move to Tuscany when she had still been feeling totally out of her depth and insecure.

Understandable really—Dervla had been less philosophical about the mix-up at the time—that a person would assume that Carla was Gianfranco's wife. The stylish Italian woman was the sort of person you expected to find married to an incredibly attractive Italian billionaire.

But he chose me, she reminded herself, sticking out her chin in an attitude of defiance.

'We should get back to the house. Carla's on her own.' She caught her lower lip between her teeth and grimaced. 'I think we've neglected her a bit this weekend,' she reflected guiltily.

The moment Angelo and Kate had arrived the two men had exchanged their suits for jeans and tee shirts and headed out onto the hills on horseback while Angelo's heavily pregnant wife had understandably been pretty much unable to talk about much else but pregnancy and birth.

'Carla's not really a woman who feels comfortable in the company of other women,' Dervla mused, thinking how the other woman became more animated when a man walked into a room—which made her efforts to seek out Dervla all the more considerate. 'And she definitely doesn't like baby talk,' she added, recalling the other woman's glazed expression and yawns.

Gianfranco threaded his thumbs into the belt loops of his jeans and turned his squinting regard on the panoramic view of the valley, drawing her a little to one side as they joined the path through the trees that led back to the house.

'But were you all right with it?' His eyes swivelled towards her, the expression in the dark depths concealed from her by the sweep of his ebony lashes. 'All the baby talk?'

Not fooled by his casual tone, Dervla knew exactly what Gianfranco was really wondering.

Was being around the heavily pregnant and glowing Kate a painful reminder of her own infertility? Did it make her mourn for the child she could never carry for the man she loved?

If she had been being strictly honest about the subject—which she never was, not even to herself—Dervla would have had to reply yes to his question. Or she would have, but, fingers crossed, things had changed. Excitement fizzed up inside her and she quickly lowered her lashes like a shield, because she knew he would see the hope she felt sure was shining in her eyes.

And now wasn't the right moment.

When she did tell Gianfranco her news she didn't want any

interruptions and cousin Carla had an instinct for walking into a room at the wrong moment!

'Of course.'

Catching her chin between his long fingers, Gianfranco tilted her face up to his.

She shifted uncomfortably under his searching scrutiny, but did not drop her eyes. After a moment he nodded, presumably satisfied by what he had seen in her face.

Dervla was amazed, but relieved—normally it was impossible to get even a half-truth past Gianfranco.

'Poor Carla,' she said as his hand fell away. 'I don't think she could get her head around the fact the staff had the weekend off and you and Angelo were cooking. I think she thought it was beneath you.'

Dervla might have once assumed the same herself when the only things she had known about the billionaire Gianfranco Bruni, socialite and hotshot ruthless financier, were the headlines containing his name she had read. It wasn't that he wasn't that man the financial pages referred to with respect, awe and in some circumstances fear, but he was more—much more.

Gianfranco was a complex man, a man with many layers. A man it would take a lifetime to understand. A man who would drive you insane with frustration while you tried!

'I have no interest in discussing Carla,' her many-layered husband remarked, oozing male arrogance as he dismissed his cousin with a click of his long fingers and turned his attention to his wife.

The raw smouldering heat in his sensuous regard sent her temperature up several degrees in the space of a single heartbeat.

'And at this moment I would much prefer that you were beneath me,' he remarked, sliding his big hands to her shoulders.

Dervla, her wide eyes melded with his smouldering dark orbs, didn't resist as he drew her towards him; molten heat pooled low in her belly and her knees gave way.

'Carla…' she faltered with one last attempt to cling to sanity and common sense.

Gianfranco just smiled, all smug male confidence, and she might have been angry with him if she hadn't been able to feel the tremors running through his body like a fever. She could forgive him for turning her into a mindless slave to desire because amazingly she did the same to him…red hair, freckles and all. The man had the oddest taste, but who was she to argue…?

Still holding her eyes with his, Gianfranco slid his hand down, grazing the contours of one small, firm breast with his knuckles before encircling it with his fingers, letting the warmth fill his palm.

There was no slow build-up; the desire that licked through like a white-hot flame was instantaneous. Dervla's head fell back, her eyelids flickering downwards across her flushed cheeks as she inhaled deeply and then released the breath on a long, fractured sigh.

As he watched her Gianfranco's arm slid supportively to her waist as her knees sagged; he pressed his mouth to the smooth column of her throat.

'Do you know how much I want you?'

Before she had any opportunity to respond to this harsh question—always supposing she had been capable of more than a whimper—he took her hand and pressed it palm down against his groin where his erection was painfully restrained by the denim.

'This much.'

Dervla's insides dissolved with primal desire, the liquid heat spreading until every hungry cell ached and throbbed with it, the pleasure bordering pain.

Gianfranco felt her gasp and shudder and when she opened her eyes and looked at him her eyes looked dark and glazed, the green almost swallowed up by the dilated pupil.

'Gianfranco, we shouldn't…' she whispered, while thinking, If we don't I'll die. I'll shrivel up and expire of sheer frustration.

Their warm breaths mingled as he tugged gently at her lower lip with his teeth. Skimming his tongue across the full, cushiony, soft, trembling, moist outline, he nuzzled his nose against hers.

'We should,' he contradicted thickly as he bent his head, fixing his warm mouth to hers. Her tongue slid sinuously against his and a ragged moan was dragged from deep in Gianfranco's chest.

'Do you know how good you feel?' he asked, cupping the curve of her bottom with his hand and dragging her hard up against him. With his free hand he began to trace the soft contours of her face, his fingertips barely touching her skin. 'I couldn't go through a day without smelling your skin, seeing your face, touching you…'

She tilted her head back and looked directly into the mesmerising heat of his eyes. She wanted, actually she ached, to say I love you, but instead she blocked the forbidden words and whispered, 'Show me how much you want me, Gianfranco.'

She saw the flame in his eyes and raised herself onto tiptoe, then slanted her mouth softly across his. As she began to pull away he released a low imprecation and, grabbing the back of her head, ground his mouth into hers. Kissing her as though he'd drain the life from her.

Lips attached, they sank entwined to the mossy floor.

A silence punctuated by soft gasps and hoarse gasps pulsed as the trees stood silent witness as they feverishly tore at each other's clothes until they lay hot bare flesh to hot bare flesh.

Gianfranco covered one hardened nipple with his mouth, causing her slender back to arch as deep darts of pleasure penetrated to the very core of her. He kissed his way down her belly as his fingers explored the soft curls at the apex of her legs before sliding deeper into her.

Feeling as though she were drowning in erotic pleasure, Dervla slid her fingers across the sweat-slick golden contours of his hard, smooth shoulders. 'Now, please!' she begged. 'Oh, my God, Gianfranco, why are you so damned good at this?' she groaned as he responded willingly to her plea.

'Look at me!' he commanded thickly as he filled her, sinking deep into her heat. 'I want to see your face.' His own face was flushed, the skin drawn tight against the strong planes and hollows of his bone structure.

Their eyes were sealed as tightly as their bodies as they moved together, both silent but for tortured breathing until a low, almost feral cry of pleasure was torn from Dervla's lips as the first wave of release hit her.

At almost the same moment she felt him pulse hotly inside her.

Stretched out lazily on the mossy floor, Gianfranco watched, one hand beneath his head, as she began to dress. Arms twisted behind her back, balanced on one leg, Dervla struggled clumsily with the clasp on her bra.

He responded to the wave of tenderness that hit him with his usual mantra of, It's just lust, a purely sexual thing, and wondered as he rode out the wave how much shelf-life that particular rationalisation had?

'You could help.'

'My expertise lies in removing undergarments. Besides, you really don't need that thing, pretty though it is,' he conceded. 'I prefer you free and unfettered, especially under a silk blouse.'

'You mean I'm flat-chested,' Dervla snapped, pretending outrage as she tore her blouse from his fingers. Actually marriage to Gianfranco had cured her of any insecurities she had about her body; he enjoyed it and had taught her to do the same.

Gianfranco laughed. 'Hardly that, *cara*! You fit in my hands just perfectly,' he reminded her, extending one hand and flexing his fingers suggestively to demonstrate the fit.

She turned her head quickly, but not before he had seen the hot fiery rush of colour to her cheeks. That she could blush now when he could still taste her on his lips, when he knew every inch of her body better than he knew his own, made him grin. 'You're blushing.'

Dervla tossed back her red hair and turned, fastening her shirt as it settled in wild rippling curls around her shoulders. 'You just like to torment me,' she charged reproachfully.

His eyes slid to her smooth, high cleavage as he levered himself upright in one fluid motion. With one hand he smoothed back her hair from her face before planting a warm, lingering kiss on her parted lips.

'It only seems fair, *cara*,' he husked, 'as you torment me.'

It was true, though the urgency of his desire had ebbed, it was never far away when he looked at her or even thought of her. He had never known anything like it.

'What are you thinking?' he asked, studying her face with the unnerving intensity that always made her feel he could see into her head and read her thoughts.

Dervla shook her head. 'I was just thinking…' She watched through her lashes, her attention drifting as he fastened the belt across his slim hips and began to button his shirt across his flat, muscle-ridged belly. 'It's just all this—'

The expressive sweep of her slim arm took in the Tuscan landscape, of rolling hills dotted with olive groves and the sensitively and expensively restored palazzo, which, with the exception of a few years when Gianfranco's father had lost it in a poker game, had been in his family since the fifteenth century.

A year ago life had been much simpler. She had been a nurse, philosophical about the fact that there was no way she could afford to get on the property ladder in London.

Now she was mistress of this vast estate and several other luxurious homes across Europe including a London Georgian town house complete with the obligatory underground pool and leisure complex, and wife of the powerful enigmatic man who earned the billions for their upkeep.

'It's so far away from my old life.'

There had been so many changes in the past year that sometimes when she caught sight of her reflection in a mirror Dervla hardly recognised the woman reflected there, and she wasn't talking designer outfits!

The changes went much deeper.

But then she hadn't actually had much choice but to adapt when she'd found herself plunged into a totally alien environment and dramatically out of her comfort zone. She'd had to develop a few new skills to cope.

And she had.

A year ago she would have laughed hysterically at the suggestion that she had the ability to get a children's hospice—funded by the charitable trust funded by Gianfranco's financial empire— from the drawing-board stage to bricks-and-mortar reality.

Similarly she would have had a panic attack at the notion that she could attend and, even more scary, host glittering events where the guests could be as diverse as politicians, Hollywood royalty and the real thing—who ever knew there were so many princes in Europe?

Maybe some of Gianfranco's—not entirely realistic in her view—confidence in her ability to do whatever he threw at her had rubbed off, because she had done both.

And become a stepmother.

A small frown puckered the smooth skin of her brow as her thoughts turned to her stepson, whom she adored.

That might have been the biggest challenge of all if Alberto had displayed even the remotest resentment of her, his new stepmother, or if Gianfranco had made it quite clear on the one occasion she had found herself in the middle of a father-son tussle that when it came to his son he made the decisions.

She had forgotten what the minor disagreement had been about, but not his words when he had referred to the incident when they were in private.

'There has been just Alberto and me for a long time now... what we have works.'

Dervla's admiration was sincere. 'I know you're a great father. I was only—'

'I will not have you undermining my authority with my son, Dervla.'

'I wasn't trying to—'

He brushed aside her protest with an impatient motion of his hand. 'Children,' he told her, apparently unaware of the insult he had offered her, 'need continuity.'

'You mean children are permanent and wives are temporary.'

His irritation was written clear in his steely stare as he retorted coldly, 'If you wish to put it that way.'

She hid her hurt behind aggression. 'You put it that way.'

His careless shrug made her resentment spill over into an unwise—she knew it the moment it left her lips—reference to his dead first wife.

'I don't suppose you told Alberto's mother it was not for ever when you proposed to her?'

His expression iced over, making him seem austere and distant. 'My marriage to Sara is not relevant. I did not marry you to give Alberto a mother.'

'I sometimes wonder why you married me at all,' she slung back childishly.

The white-hot blaze in his eyes as he grabbed her by the shoulders and dragged her up against his long, lean body made her knees fold as he gave his driven response to her question.

'I married you because you wouldn't be my mistress, because I couldn't think straight without you in my bed and because I will not share you with another man.'

No mention of love, but he kissed her and she told herself she didn't care. About three seconds later she stopped thinking entirely.

Dervla sighed. It was always that way the moment Gianfranco

touched her: her principles and pride vaporised. Which was why she had ended up married to a man who never even pretended he loved her, though for one split second when he had proposed her mind had made that understandable assumption.

'But you barely know me!' she protested. 'It takes time to fall in love, Gianfranco and—' She stopped, the colour seeping from her face as the truth—as she saw it then—hit her.

Time had not the first thing to do with falling in love. And for some people it actually didn't take long at all…in her case it had taken about a second, and now it seemed that amazingly it had been the same for Gianfranco…? Only he had had the sense to recognise it.

She lifted her dazed eyes to his lean, devastatingly handsome face and thought, I really do love you. A shuddering sigh left her parted lips; a smile of wondering joy spread across her face.

Gianfranco, she saw, was smiling too, only his smile twisted his mobile lips into a cynical grimace and left his incredible eyes unusually cold.

'I am not looking for love.'

Her face remained frozen in the smile, but the light had gone out of her eyes as he expanded on the theme.

'If such a thing actually exists…?'

'You don't think so, I take it.'

One dark brow moved in the direction of his hairline and he sketched a sardonic smile. 'Outside fairy tales? Do you know how many marriages actually last more than a few years?'

'So how long do you propose our—our hypothetical marriage will last?'

'You cannot fix a specific time when there are so many unknown variables.'

God, and they say romance is dead! 'So when you say for better or worse, what you actually mean is until the gloss wears off or something better comes along?'

'You think it's somehow more courageous and noble to stay

in a marriage because of a sense of obligation?' Lip curled, he shook his head. 'That's not nobility. At best it's habit, at worst it's laziness and fear. I'm being a realist. You might prefer me to trot out the clichés about us being fated to be together through eternity?'

'People are. My parents had been married thirty-five years when they were killed.'

'An accident?'

'The coach they were travelling in went across the central reservation of the motorway and hit a lorry coming in the opposite direction. Ten people were killed, including my parents.'

'You were how old?'

'Eighteen, in my first year of nurse training."

'I am sorry, and I am glad your parents had a happy marriage, but I cannot see into the future. I have no idea what I will feel in five, ten years' time, but I know what I feel now.

'Now,' he told her, in a voice that made every single nerve ending in her body sigh, 'I want you.'

That had been a year ago and he still wanted her, and any future plans he spoke of included her.

What are you going to do when he doesn't and they don't?

Fear tightened and clenched inside her and with a small cry she turned and buried her head in Gianfranco's chest. 'I'm happy!' she declared defiantly.

Startled by her abrupt action, Gianfranco stared down for a moment at the top of her head before lifting a hand to stroke a fiery curl, stretching it and then letting it spring back softly into shape.

'Happy?'

Dervla felt his hands on her shoulders and burrowed deeper into him, her eyes closed, feeling the solid warmth of his lean, hard male body seep into her as his arms folded across her ribcage.

'Yes, I'm happy.'

Everyone had a different recipe for happiness, but she knew that hers had one vital ingredient: Gianfranco.

So things might not be perfect, the alternative was no Gianfranco. It was an alternative she could not bring herself to contemplate; it was the reason she had said yes when he proposed.

Gianfranco prised her face from his shirt. One big hand framed the side of her face, the other sliding into the lush silky curls on her nape to cradle her skull as he scanned her face.

An image superimposed itself in his head of Dervla's face when she had told him that she couldn't marry him because she wasn't able to have children.

Dio mio, I'm about as sensitive as that stone, he thought, kicking a wedged rock free with the toe of his shoe.

How, he asked himself, did you expect her to feel, when you have her spend the entire weekend with a heavily pregnant woman who babbles incessantly about babies? Of course she cared more than she pretended.

Dervla had been up front about it from the beginning.

He had not been so honest in his response.

He had seen the gratitude shining in her eyes when he had promised her that her inability to conceive made no difference to him; she clearly hadn't believed a word he said, but he hadn't made any real push to dissuade her from her clear belief in his nobility.

Contrary to what she thought, there was no sacrifice on his part; when she had told him of this tragedy in her life his reaction had been relief!

Relief he would never now need to have that awkward conversation—the one where he would have to dredge up his past mistakes.

'Happy? So that,' he teased lightly as he blotted with his thumb the sparkling tear that was sliding down her cheek, 'is a tear of joy?'

Dervla didn't respond to his comment. Instead she tilted her head and asked, 'Are you happy, Gianfranco?'

'What is happy?'

She saw the trace of irritation in his face at the question, and thought, If you were happy you wouldn't need to ask.

'I would be happier,' he said, taking her hand, 'if Carla decides to go home this evening.'

CHAPTER TWO

GIANFRANCO'S wish was not granted.

When they got back to the house Carla, wearing a swimsuit encrusted with sequins and quite obviously designed more for displaying her perfect body beside a pool than swimming in, asked Gianfranco if she could beg a seat in his helicopter the next morning.

'I thought you had things to get back to.'

'No, I'm all yours,' the older woman responded, apparently oblivious to the strong hint. 'And the staff are back so you won't need to vanish into the kitchen. You're both so eccentric,' she murmured, shaking her head before pleading with a pretty smile for Gianfranco to apply some sunscreen to her back.

Dervla stiffened, her hands balling instinctively into fists as an image of Gianfranco's hands on the other woman's warm, smooth skin formed in her head.

'I don't think you're in danger of burning, Carla. It's six-thirty.'

With a quick smile at Carla, Dervla followed him indoors. 'Will you not be so rude to Carla,' she hissed.

He arched a brow. 'You wish me to put cream on other women? I think not. I saw your face. You'd have pushed her into the pool if I'd tried.' He did not sound displeased by the discovery.

The colour flew to Dervla's cheeks. 'No, I'd have pushed you into the pool, but this is Carla—she doesn't mean anything by it.' Be tolerant, Dervla, be tolerant. 'She's like that with all men.'

He gave a grimace of fastidious distaste. 'You mean she comes on to all men.'

Dervla's eyes flew wide. She pressed her hand to her stomach feeling suddenly nauseous. 'She's never…with you, has she?'

'A gentleman does not speak of such things.'

'So that leaves you free to spill the dirt.'

Gianfranco threw back his head and laughed. 'She is really not my type, *cara*,' he promised, lifting a hand to stroke her cheek. 'And you need not worry about her feelings. She has the skin of a rhino. Short of showing her the door, we're stuck with her until tomorrow. I suppose we'll just have to grin and bear it.'

During dinner Gianfranco showed very little inclination to follow his own advice, so it was left to Dervla to supply the extra smiles.

By the time the Italian woman was midway through a lengthy description of the famous people she had rubbed shoulders with at a recent celebrity auction Dervla's facial muscles were aching from the marathon.

'What charity was the auction for?' she asked when Carla paused for breath.

'For…?' The older woman looked at her blankly for a moment.

'The charity it was raising money for?'

'I really can't recall.'

Dervla bit her lip, and didn't dare look at Gianfranco, she knew he'd make her laugh.

'Did I mention that I spoke to the prince? A charming man.'

Before Dervla had a chance to adopt an appropriate expression of polite enquiry Gianfranco cut in with a dry, 'Yes, you did, Carla—several times.'

Dervla shot her husband a look of warning from beneath the sweep of her lashes and said brightly to fill the awkward silence, 'Are you sure you won't have some of this lemon tart, Carla?'

'No, no pudding, I'm watching my weight.' The glance she slid the second slice on Dervla's plate suggested that she thought Dervla ought to be doing the same. 'But, you could lend me your husband, just for a few minutes. Boring financial stuff…' She angled a look of enquiry at Gianfranco. 'If it wouldn't be too much of a bother…?'

There was a pause and for one awful moment Dervla thought Gianfranco was going to say yes, it would be too much of a bother, when he got to his feet, his attitude more polite resignation than eagerness. 'If it's urgent?'

'Well, you probably won't think it is, but I have been worried.'

'Would you like to come to the study?' His enquiring glance slid towards Dervla.

'I'll wait here.'

Carla smoothed her creaseless skirt down over her slim hips and patted Dervla's hand. 'Don't worry, I won't keep him a minute.'

The minute Carla had spoken of stretched into an hour while Dervla sat alone at the dinner table drinking coffee. When the maid came in she refused the offer of another pot and told the girl with a smile she could clear away.

Another five minutes and she decided she might as well go to bed. As she passed the door of Gianfranco's study she heard some very unfinancial-sounding laughter before she shouted her intention of retiring.

'I'll be up in a moment!' Gianfranco called out.

It turned out his grasp of time was just as sketchy as Carla's. It was actually midnight when Gianfranco finally did join her in their bedroom. Hearing his footsteps in the corridor outside, Dervla leapt into bed, picking up a magazine from the table on her way.

'What did she want?'

Conscious that this was one of those situations where it would be very easy to sound like a jealous wife, Dervla was careful that nothing in her manner suggested her interest in Gianfranco's response to her question was anything but tepid.

Actually she had spent the past hour pacing up and down, her eyes drawn continually to the hands on the clock. It wasn't that she was jealous as such of Carla, and she was sure that Gianfranco did not think of the older woman in that way, but they had a history, a history she was excluded from, memories she did not share.

Carla had been a close friend of Alberto's mother, Sara. Had the conversation in the library turned to Sara?

While every snippet of information she'd gleaned from Carla had only confirmed her suspicion that Sara had been the love of Gianfranco's life, some hitherto unsuspected streak of masochism in her made Dervla hungry for the details even though she was tortured by every new proof of how special their love had been.

Gianfranco gave a disgruntled snort. 'Some stuff about shares, hardly urgent.'

The same could not be said of his desire to join his wife in their bed. The light from the bedside lamp picked out the gold in her burnished hair and made the nightgown she wore almost transparent. His body hardened as he looked at her; her slim, supple curves never failed to arouse him.

'Finally,' he said, walking towards the bed where she sat hugging her knees, 'I have you all to myself.'

She tilted her head and reminded him, 'This weekend was your idea.'

'It was a bad idea.' Slipping the buttons on his shirt, he sat down beside her on the bed. He reached for the magazine in his way and Dervla, catching a glimpse of the cover, tried to snatch it away.

'What are you reading that you don't want me to see?'

'Nothing, nothing, let me have it, Gianfranco.'

The anxiety in her voice made him frown. He leaned back, the magazine in his hand, and turned it over. His teasing smile faded. It was a medical journal.

Dervla sighed. 'Oh, all right, I didn't want to tell you this way, but the doctor suggested I read this article…'

'Article?' He glanced down. The front cover announced the contents included the latest research on a new drug for breast cancer.

It took his mind a microsecond to make the next sickening leap. He felt as if someone had just reached inside his chest and placed an icy hand around his heart.

'What's wrong?' he asked, telling himself that his feelings were not important, this was about Dervla and he had to be strong and stay positive for her.

Her eyes slid from his, her lashes brushing her smooth cheeks as she turned her head. 'Nothing. Nothing's wrong.'

He cupped her chin in his hand, drawing her face up to him as he moved closer to her on the bed.

'You are a terrible liar.' Please, God, let this not be happening. 'Look, whatever it is we can face it together… It is never hopeless—they are coming up with new cures for…' He stopped and took a deep breath. He had to stay positive for her sake. 'Cancer is just a word.'

She gave a small cry of denial, her eyes widening in horrified comprehension. 'No…no, it's nothing like that. I promise you, Gianfranco, I'm not ill.'

'You're not?'

When she shook her head positively he released a long sigh, his shoulders slumping as the most intense relief he had ever felt in his life washed over him.

There was, he realised, a degree of truth in the old adage that said you didn't know how much you cared for something until you were faced with the prospect of losing it—or her!

'You're sure?'

She caught hold of both his hands and, drawing herself up to her knees, rubbed her nose against his. 'Totally.'

He jerked her hard towards him and kissed her fiercely on

her soft, parted lips. 'If you ever do that to me again,' he promised when he finally released her, 'I will throttle you.' His eyes went to the slim pale length of her throat. Desire thickened his voice as he added, 'Do you understand?'

Dervla sank back onto her heels, looking flushed and deliciously tousled but not unduly concerned by the growled threat, and nodded.

'I understand.'

'So as we have established you are not dying on me—' despite the flippancy in his voice he was forced to shove his hands in his pockets to hide the fact they were still shaking '—just what are you doing reading that?'

Dervla looked at him through her lashes, her green eyes sparkling with suppressed excitement. 'You read it,' she suggested, opening the magazine and stabbing the page with her finger before handing it to him.

It didn't take him long to skim the relevant article. When he'd finished he closed the magazine and put it on the bed. The article discussed the success rate of a brand-new fertility treatment that would, it suggested, offer hope to women who previously had none.

'Well?' she asked excitedly. 'What do you think? They're looking for suitable women for the next clinical trial. I know there's no guarantee, but—'

He cut across her. 'This is what you have worked yourself into such a state about?' Shaking his head, he reached for her and she came willingly warm and soft into his arms. He held her close, his fingers meshed in her shiny, sweet-smelling hair, her head pressed to his heart as he reminded her, 'I told you, Dervla, before we married that I don't want children.'

'I know what you said and it was kind—'

'It was not kind; it was true.'

She pulled away and tilted her face up to his, her smooth brow furrowed and her expression shocked as she impatiently blotted a solitary tear from her cheek with the back of her hand.

Far from swaying or softening his attitude, previously women's tears had evoked irritation in Gianfranco, but Dervla had never used her tears as a weapon to manipulate him.

She felt things more deeply than anyone he had ever met. Her emotions were incredibly close to the surface, her face as easy for him to read as a neon sign. But despite her almost unnerving transparency she did her crying in private.

'You *really* don't want children.' She shook her head, a frown pulling her arched brows into a bemused straight line as she added as if speaking to herself, 'No, that can't be right. I've seen you with Alberto and with the other children. You're great and—'

'A baby is a lot of work. Babies kill your social life, *cara*. Call me selfish—' better get that in before she did '—but I don't want to come home to a wife who is too exhausted to do more than crawl into bed.'

She looked at him as though he had grown a second head and it wasn't a particularly attractive one.

'You don't mean that, Gianfranco.'

'It is not me who has changed my mind,' he reminded her harshly. 'It is you.'

'I thought that you'd be pleased that there was a chance,' she choked in a voice thick with tears and disillusion. 'Kate is giving Angelo a baby, I want to—'

'We are not Kate and Angelo. The cases are not similar.'

He watched the pinpricks of bright blood appear on the quivering curve of her lower lip as she released it to say in a voice wiped clean of all expression, 'Do you think I don't know that?'

'I already have a son.' A son he would gladly have laid down his life to protect…just as his mother had.

It was this knowledge that gave him the strength to withstand the appeal in her eyes. Of course he knew that nobody blamed him for Sara's death and rationally he recognised it had not been his fault, but the fact remained that had he not been irresponsible enough to get her pregnant, had he not cajoled her into marriage with promises of a luxurious life-style and persuaded her against a termination, she would be alive today.

Dervla's full lower lip wobbled and there was a tremor in her voice as she said bleakly, 'But *we* could have a baby together. I don't have a son. I don't have a baby. The doctor said there have been incredible advances in IVF over the last few years.'

'And you went to see a doctor behind my back...' Gianfranco blocked his growing feelings of guilt with anger.

'Don't look at me like that, Gianfranco.'

'Like what?' he asked her coldly.

She slung him an exasperated look. 'I think you'd have been happier if I'd just told you I was having an affair!' she accused.

Another man—that was funny... Her lips twitched and a burble of borderline hysteria escaped them, causing the fine lines of tension and anxiety around her mouth to briefly smooth out.

Gianfranco watched her, his face like stone. Dervla being touched by another man did not make him feel like laughing or even smiling. It ignited a rage deep inside him.

Dervla sighed and shook her head in a slow negative motion. She made a conscious effort to lower the escalating antagonism.

'I wasn't going behind your back—just wanted some facts before I discussed it with you. I didn't see any reason to raise your hopes, and he said that—'

Gianfranco cut across her; he didn't want to hear what any doctor had said. It had been a doctor who had told him that the diabetes that Sara had developed during pregnancy was no cause for concern. Gestational diabetes, he had explained, was common but rarely a problem after the birth.

And like a fool he had believed him.

Far from vanishing after the birth, Sara's condition had pro-gressed to full insulin-dependent diabetes requiring daily injections. And again he had been won over by the confident medical assertion that there was no reason that Sara could not live a full normal life.

It had been three months later that he had buried Sara, who had died of an accidental overdose of insulin.

'I thought our marriage was based on transparency?'

'No our marriage—' She bit back, pushing herself off the bed… God, if she didn't she'd have strangled him! 'What about what I want, Gianfranco? What I need?' Pushing her arms into a robe, she turned and threw him a look of challenge.

'I thought I gave you what you want and need.'

'I want this baby.'

'There is no baby, Dervla.'

'There could be, there could be!' she wailed, frustrated by his refusal to even consider what she was saying.

'I know people who have been down the IVF route. It took over their lives, put a lot of strain on their relationship, not to mention the emotional and physical strain being pumped full of chemicals has on the woman.'

'Some people think it's worth it…and if you never even try you'd always wonder.'

'That is not a route I wish ever to go down. Besides, from what you told me the chances of you getting pregnant would be remote.' If it took brutal to get his point across, so be it.

Dervla pressed her clenched fists tight against her stomach; she felt physically sick.

'But there is a chance.' She couldn't believe that Gianfranco couldn't see she had to take it. The icy hand inside her chest tightened as she watched him slowly shake his head.

'There is no use begging, Dervla. I will not give you a baby.'

Anger flooded through her, releasing adrenaline into her bloodstream. Maybe it wasn't a baby he didn't want—it was *her* baby. 'Then maybe I'll find myself someone who will.'

If he had reacted angrily, if he had done almost anything but thrown back his head and laughed, she might have calmed down…but he did laugh.

'You think I wouldn't?'

He stopped laughing.

Dervla shivered as their eyes connected. She had never seen his eyes look so cold.

'I know you wouldn't.' Because if he caught a man within sniffing distance of her he would make sure they never sniffed again!

Dervla's eyes narrowed to icy green slits. 'Is that a fact?' she said in a conversational tone. 'What do you know? Infallible Gianfranco Bruni turns out not to know everything after all.'

'What are you doing?' he asked as she began to rush around the room erratically flinging open doors and drawers and flinging the contents she extracted into a bag.

'I'm packing.'

His patrician features tight, he gave a contemptuous sneer. 'You're being ridiculous.' She wouldn't go.

She went to the drawer and pulled out her passport. 'No, I'm finally not being ridiculous. Marrying you, I must have been mad! You're the most selfish man I have ever met,' she choked. 'I'll take a car. I'll leave it at the airport.'

CHAPTER THREE

THERE had been no question of where Dervla would go.

When she was in trouble it had been totally predictable where, or rather who, she would bolt to, sure of a welcome and equally sure her best friend Sue wouldn't push her for explanations until she was ready.

Her actions were actually so predictable that she couldn't even pretend that Gianfranco's silence was due to his inability to locate her. He would know her destination without cause to use the mental powers some people nervously suggested bordered on the paranormal.

She couldn't even picture him desperately searching for her. The only thing Gianfranco was desperately doing was ignoring the fact she existed, ignoring the fact he had a wife.

She was considering his seeming indifference to her flight when the phone rang.

For a moment Dervla froze and stared at it as if it were a striking snake.

It would serve him right if she ignored it.

Even before the thought was half formed she literally dived for it. Her hand shook as she lifted the receiver and raised it to her ear.

'Hello.' She was barely able to force the quivering word past the emotional occlusion in her aching throat.

The pathetically eager smile on her face faded dramatically as the voice the other end assured her that they were not selling anything before launching into their slick sales pitch.

Slender shoulders hunched, Dervla sank disconsolately onto Sue's sagging sofa, ingrained good manners making it impossible for her to hang up. So she let the disembodied voice describe uninterrupted the superiority of the double-glazing they were selling and resisted the temptation to enquire bitterly if this marvellous system, which could apparently do anything, could make a man love you.

Or, failing that, make a person fall out of love? Yeah, that would work and make them a lot of money; love really wasn't what it was cracked up to be.

'So our sales representatives are in your area next week. Would you like one to call?'

Dervla roused herself from her bitter reflections and said apologetically, 'Sorry, I'm not the home owner. I'm just camping on the sofa because I walked out of my marriage.' And my husband shows no sign of giving a damn. For all she knew he could be celebrating his freedom. Maybe not alone?

The startled intake of breath on the other end almost made her smile as she put the receiver down. She glanced at the clock and could not believe it was still only three o'clock.

Each agonising minute of the interminable day had felt like an hour. The wistful ache became a pain as she allowed thoughts of Gianfranco to invade her thoughts.

You walked, she reminded herself.

And he hadn't followed. She'd never forgive him for that.

What are you going to do, Dervla? she asked herself. Spend the rest of your life two feet from this phone just in case he decides to remember he has a wife? It was pretty clear that Gianfranco was getting on with his life, and wasn't it about time she did the same thing?

One thing was certain: if she wanted to retain a crumb of self-respect she couldn't sit around in this pathetic needy way.

She was going to have to start making plans for her future as a single woman. Fortunately she was well qualified so there would be no problem earning a living, even if that did mean some agency work initially.

She picked up the TV control and, with about as much enthusiasm as she could muster for the prospect of picking up the threads of her old life, clicked on the TV.

The face of a smartly dressed woman fronting the news channel filled the screen. She looked to Dervla like someone whose personal life was not a total messy disaster area, or maybe that wasn't possible?

Maybe personal lives were by definition messy?

"On the first anniversary of the tragedy…"

Dervla's eyes widened as the serene newscaster was replaced by an image reminiscent of a war zone—total devastation filled the screen, torn metal, screaming sirens, then they cut to a dazed-looking man with blood on his face praising the emergency services.

"A remembrance service is being held," said the voice-over.

Dervla's expression went blank with shock. Gianfranco as a survivor had received an invitation to that service, but, a firm believer in living in the present and looking to the future not the past—a slightly ironic attitude for someone who had never recovered from the death of his first wife—he had politely turned it down.

I forgot… How, she wondered, loosing a small incredulous laugh, was that possible?

How could she forget the day that changed so many lives? And not just those of the victims. There was a ripple effect with such tragedies, though in her own case the ripple that had caught her up and carried her as far as Italy had been more of a tidal wave!

It had officially been her day off, but once the hospital she had worked at had been put on red alert following the detonation of a bomb in a crowded street she, like other essential off-duty staff, had been called in.

By the time she had arrived the staff on duty in the unit had already freed up as many beds as they could, transferring those fit enough to general wards to make way for the casualties.

Young Alberto Bruni had been one of those casualties and Dervla had been designated his nurse. Glancing at the clock just as the swing doors were pushed open to admit the trolley bearing the youngster from Theatre, she had been shocked to realise that she had already been on duty eight hours straight.

'Dervla, when did you last take a break?'

Dervla turned to smile at the concerned face of the charge nurse, John Stewart. The bags beneath his blue eyes had doubled their capacity since yesterday. Dervla wondered if she looked as tired as he did.

'My patient is just arriving from Theatre, John. I'll wait until he's settled.' She glanced down at the name on the notes that had just arrived. 'Bruni,' she read out loud. 'Another tourist, do you think?'

'Maybe. It sounds Italian.'

Dervla's brow puckered as she nibbled thoughtfully on her full lower lip. 'I wonder if he speaks English?' she said aloud, trying to anticipate any problems, not even suspecting that six feet five inches of major life-changing problem was at that moment walking into the room.

'Well, if he doesn't,' the charge nurse said, lowering his voice as he inclined his head towards the open door, 'he does. The father, do you suppose…? Now that is a turn-up for the books,' he observed, not looking thrilled with the development.

'Who…?' Dervla turned and stopped, her eyes widening as she saw the cause of the tired charge nurse's comments.

The cause was actually pretty hard to miss—definitely not the fade-into-a-crowd type! Several inches over six feet, the man who walked beside the trolley moved with a riveting fluid grace Dervla normally associated with athletes or dancers.

The dust and dirt coating his face and hair proclaimed him to be one of the walking wounded and though his clothing was filthy and bloodstained he wore it with such assurance that you only noticed this after you had noticed the man who wore it.

For a moment she stared, jaw ajar, and she wasn't the only person present to forget her clinical objectivity! He was quite simply the most utterly incredible-looking man Dervla had ever seen. She had only ever read about men who looked like him—in actual fact she had read about this man, because her young patient turned out to be the son of none other than Gianfranco Bruni.

And pretty much everyone in the Western world had read about him!

Standing a few feet away, it wasn't hard to see why he fascinated the media. There were probably any number of Italian aristocrats who could trace their lineage back for centuries, but very few had built a financial empire out of virtually nothing. Even fewer would have matched up to the average person's image of what such a man should look like.

Gianfranco Bruni did.

He had the hauteur, the flashing eyes, chiselled photogenic cheekbones and sensual sexy mouth. He had the stunning body, muscular, tall and broad-shouldered.

Then he had the less definable qualities, namely raw, undiluted sex appeal. Unwilling to admit even to herself that it was this latter quality that had caused her brain to momentarily stall, Dervla put down to exhaustion the light-headed sensation she experienced as she looked at him?

'Is that really Gianfranco Bruni?' For once the media hadn't exaggerated when they had extolled his looks.

The man beside her laughed. 'Well, if he isn't he's his twin brother. Be sure you take care with phone enquiries, Dervla.

Once the press get onto this they'll be all over us like a damned rash. And if he gives you any problems refer him to me.'

'Don't worry, John, I can handle him.' Laughably she actually believed it at the time!

But she wasn't the first to make that fatal error, though she would have preferred to lose her shirt to him than her heart.

'Just do your job, Dervla, and leave the politics to the men in suits. Talking of which…I'll go and deal with those two,' he said, nodding unenthusiastically in the direction of the two high-ranking hospital administrators who were shadowing the Italian.

'They're probably trying to hit him for a donation to the kidney unit.' Dervla was only half joking.

'Not while I'm in charge, they're not.' He stopped as the nurse who had escorted the boy approached, and demanded irritably, 'Why didn't you get the father to wait outside?'

'I did,' she protested, looking flustered. 'Well, I tried,' she corrected. 'But he, well…' she glanced towards the tall Italian and shrugged, rolling her eyes '…what was I meant to do when he ignored me? Sit on him?'

Dervla's eyes followed the direction of the theatre nurse's gaze. She could imagine there were any number of females who lacked her professional objectivity who would jump at the chance to sit on him!

Her patient's father was standing motionless beside the stationary trolley, surveying the room. You definitely got the sense that his present inactivity was not the norm for him. The high-powered financier had presumably not got his billions by being someone who did relaxed or passive on a regular basis.

Dervla flashed the other girl a look of sympathy. 'She's got a point, John.' This was clearly not a man who responded to requests unless he wanted to.

You could tell just by looking at him that he was one of those individuals hard-wired to take control. The message couldn't have been clearer had he walked in with 'dominant male' stamped on his broad, intelligent, bloodstained forehead.

Not that a forehead could be termed intelligent as such.

But eyes were another matter. And the diamond-hard eyes through which the Italian had surveyed the room as he paused there in the entrance made a cut-throat razor look dull-edged.

Pretty astounding, considering he had been through an experience that would have had most people lying sedated in a hospital bed!

As she stared curiously his sweeping scrutiny reached her.

Dervla's body and mind reacted to the brush of those dark eyes set in the perfect symmetry of his chiselled golden skinned face in a similar way it might to a jolt of neat electricity.

A wave of scalding heat washed over her fair skin, then receded leaving her feeling shivery as she reacted helplessly to the predatory sexual magnetism this incredible-looking man exuded.

Was it her imagination or had his glance lingered longer than required…? But then a split second could seem longer when you were holding your breath, and she had been!

Once his glance moved on Dervla's brain started functioning again and she was able to put her mortifying reaction in perspective.

Obviously it had had more to do with fatigue than anything hormonal. He wasn't even the type of man she found attractive. She never had gone for arrogance or the whole smouldering Latin thing. If it had been otherwise she might have been more concerned about the little aftershocks she experienced as she approached him—shocks presented in the form of pulse racing and uncomfortable shivery sensations.

As she reached his side she realised that the theatre nurse hadn't been the only person he'd ignored in the hospital, because she couldn't believe nobody had suggested—pretty forcibly— that he have the gaping wound on his forehead sutured.

And goodness only knew what lay concealed, besides golden tautly muscled skin, beneath his torn and bloodstained clothes. Give that shirt a tug and she'd find out, Dervla thought, registering the one button stopping the garment being open to the waist. As it was it really left very little to the imagination!

If a person had been asked to judge from his body alone what the Italian billionaire did for a living she suspected a lot would have plumped for professional athlete.

He had the natural grace and the sleek muscle definition that few beyond those whose livelihood depended on it ever achieved.

A man who spent his life making money might be expected to carry a bit of excess weight around the middle. Staring at his she could see that it was washboard-flat.

Dragging her eyes upwards, her cheeks gently tinged with colour, she felt her tension level rise as her eyes connected with eyes that were startlingly dark, heavily fringed by a screen of jet lashes and hard as diamonds.

She wondered guiltily if he'd seen her ogling—not an ideal first impression.

'Hello, I'm Dervla Smith.' She flashed her practised soothing smile and had no response. 'I'll be the nurse looking after Alberto. Second cubicle,' she said, nodding to the waiting porter. 'If you'd like to wait outside someone will come and get you when Alberto is settled.'

'No.'

Dervla blinked. 'Pardon…?'

'Are you hard of hearing?' he wondered sardonically.

Her smile wobbled as she reminded herself that people reacted to shock and trauma in many ways. Some became aggressive, some became obnoxious—occasionally you came across one who combined the two. Then again maybe this was standard billionaire behaviour…?

Not that it made any difference to the way she'd treat him. As far as she was concerned he was her patient's father. His bank balance was no more relevant than the preposterous length of his eyelashes—and actually far less distracting.

'I said no, I would not like to wait outside.' Leaving her standing there, he began to follow the porters.

Mouth twisted into a rueful grimace, she watched his broad back retreat. Well, you really established your authority there, Dervla. He definitely knows who is boss.

John, having ejected the men in suits, walked by and raised an enquiring brow. 'All right, Dervla?'

'Absolutely.'

Her annoyance with the Italian drained away as she approached the bed and saw his expression in profile as he looked down at the unconscious figure of his child. She had seen gut-wrenching fear before and watched people struggle to contain it.

A wave of empathy washed over her—Gianfranco Bruni was living his nightmare.

CHAPTER FOUR

THE dark eyes swivelled briefly in Dervla's direction as she untangled an IV line before Gianfranco's attention returned to the boy in the bed.

'I understand it will be some time before he regains consciousness…?' His low, slightly accented voice had a tactile quality that sent an illicit shiver along Dervla's susceptible nerve endings.

She was accustomed to dealing with tearful, distraught relatives, but this man did not fit neatly into that category—or, she suspected, any other!

Superficially at least he appeared utterly composed.

She might have called him cold if she hadn't been given that brief glimpse behind the mask of clinical composure. She couldn't see his face as he leant forward and brushed a strand of dark hair from his son's waxy brow, but she could see the tell-tale tremor in his long tapering brown fingers.

'These things are hard to predict.'

'Try,' he recommended tersely. 'And please take that expression off your face,' he said without actually looking at her.

Dervla started guiltily and wondered if eyes in the back of his head were the secret to his success?

'I do not need sympathy. I need answers.' His clinical detachment slipped another notch as he added angrily, 'Neither do I need you to dumb down for my benefit. I may not have a medical degree but I am not an imbecile!'

Dervla was not offended by his manner. She had dealt with anxious parents before, though admittedly not one who looked like a fallen angel.

She was pretty sure that if she had met him outside the precincts of the hospital in a non-professional capacity—a pretty unlikely scenario as they inhabited different worlds—she might have found Gianfranco Bruni overwhelming.

But that was not the case now.

And even if it had been she could hide any inappropriate feelings behind her professional mask, because here it didn't matter how much money he had or how many politicians or film stars he classed as close personal friends. Here and now he was a father worried out of his skull about his son and it was her job to make sure the son got well and the father stopped worrying.

Dervla was good at her job.

'I'm sure the doctors have already explained the situation.'

Her soothing tone that calmed so many patients had no visible effect on this man. He silenced her with an imperious movement of his head. 'The doctors talk and say nothing!' He sounded disgusted.

'And you thought I'd be easier to bully. Sorry, but it doesn't work that way.'

He raised an astonished ebony brow and muttered something under his breath in Italian. Dervla struggled to maintain her serene smile as that heavy-lidded gaze moved across her face as though he was seeing her for the first time.

She got the distinct impression he wasn't overly impressed by what he saw.

'You think I'm a bully?'

It was pretty obvious that he didn't actually give a damn what she thought of him. She was starting to doubt he cared what anyone thought about him. But he did sound genuinely curious.

'I wouldn't know about that, but I do know that you're a worried father.' Her eyes softened as they swept across the face of the unconscious youngster. 'He really is in the right place, you know.'

She turned her head in time to see emotion flicker in the back of those spectacular obsidian eyes, but a moment later as they fixed on her there was no residual softness reflected in the dark surface.

'Pity, Nurse, he were not in the right place at two this afternoon.' He inhaled, turned his head and passed a hand across his eyes as though to banish nightmare images that were playing in his head.

'Look, is there anyone I can contact for you?' In her opinion this was not a time when anyone should be alone.

'I am more than capable of making a phone call should I need to.'

It was clear he was also capable of being even more abrasively rude if he felt she had trespassed on personal territory. 'Fine.' She accepted the latest snub with a smile but risked another by adding, 'Alberto's mother or…?'

The hand dropped and he looked at her coldly, condensing what must have been a heartbreaking event in his life into a short factual sentence. 'Alberto's mother is dead.'

'I'm sorry.'

'And to save you the bother, it's not a juicy titbit that the papers will shell out for. Old news, I'm afraid. The media have already done the story to death.'

It took a few seconds for the implication to sink in. When it did the angry colour flew to her cheeks.

With a forced smile she levelled her glittering gaze on his face. 'I can assure you, Mr Bruni, that like myself all the hospital staff here take patient confidentiality very seriously.'

'I made you angry.'

He sounded surprised… Good God, how did the wretched man expect her to feel? He'd just virtually said she'd sell her soul if the price was right! She compressed her generous lips into a tight smile. 'I'm not angry,' she lied.

Her denial appeared to amuse him, if the cynical curve of his sensual mouth could be termed a smile. 'The voice was good but the eyes need some work…they are very expressive.' His glance lingered briefly on her wide emerald-green eyes. 'No insult was intended, Nurse…' his heavy lidded eyes swerved to the name badge on her heaving bosom before he inserted '…Smith.'

His cynical drawl got so far under Dervla's skin that she really struggled to remember that he was a man in an emotionally vulnerable position in need of sensitive handling.

'It's nothing personal,' he added. 'Everyone has their price.'

'If I believed that, I'd be too depressed to get up in the morning, Mr Bruni. There's a coffee machine in the relatives' sitting room,' she added, hoping that coffee was an impersonal enough subject to suit this cynical man with the obvious allergy to sympathy. 'If you'd like to go there while I make Alberto comfortable…?'

'I would have thought that making my son comfortable with half a dozen tubes sticking out of him is well nigh impossible.'

'They do tea and hot chocolate too. Though it's actually pretty hard to tell the difference,' she admitted. 'But it's wet.'

'Tea…*per amor di Dio!*' he echoed, looking at her as though she were a raving lunatic. 'The British think tea cures all things. Are you sure that's not what you're drip-feeding him?' he asked, his eyes shifting to the bag of fluid suspended above his son's bed. 'I require no refreshments and I prefer it when you are trying to antagonise me than when you are trying to mother me.'

'I wasn't trying to antagonise you!' she protested, then added belatedly, 'Or mother you.' Being forced to talk to the back of his head gave her the opportunity to see that underneath the layer of dust, blood and grime his hair was black as ebony and silky straight. It was the sort of hair that might be pleasant to run your fingers through—if, of course, it were on someone else's head.

'Actually I was just being tactful. It will be easier to attend to your son if you are…well, not here.' She was barely able to repress a shudder at the thought of those dark eyes watching her every move.

He turned his head. The smile on his lips did not reach his eyes. 'I admire your candour,' he said, sounding anything but admiring. 'And let me pay you the compliment of being equally frank. I am not even slightly concerned with making your life easier, or hospital protocol.'

Big surprise!

By sheer will she kept her expression impassive. It was hard. She found it impossible not to be moved by his obvious devotion to his son, but, God, this man was hard going.

'Relatives very often find it distressing to watch their loved ones—'

He cut across her in a voice that leaked impatience, the same impatience that was evident in the tension in every sinew of his long, lean body. 'It was distressing to be required to dig my son out of the rubble.'

The reminder of the ordeal he had so recently endured made Dervla ashamed of losing her objectivity. There was no excuse in her eyes for allowing personal feelings, especially antagonism, to influence her in the workplace.

'It must have been terrible,' she said softly.

Appearing not to hear her soft comment, Gianfranco held up his hands and stared at his long fingers ingrained with dirt and blood for several seconds before he shook his head.

Wondering what images he was trying to banish, Dervla felt a surge of sympathy that she knew better than to express.

'Watching you take his blood pressure—' he said, switching his attention back to her so abruptly that Dervla flinched '—is something I feel able to deal with without passing out.'

She wished she could share his confidence. The man was obviously operating on adrenaline, and will-power. The former at least was not inexhaustible and at some point it was going to hit him.

Not yet, it seemed.

She watched as he rotated his broad shoulders as if to iron out the kinks in his spine, then with a fluid shrug he drew himself up to his full height.

Forced to tilt her head back to meet his eyes, Dervla was struck even more forcibly than ever by the overwhelming nature of the Italian's physical presence.

He levelled a thoughtful gaze at her, holding her eyes for several uncomfortable—as her sweaty palms attested—moments, and then without a word took hold of the chair drawn up to the bed and dragged it back a few feet to give her clear access.

'I will not get in your way, but I will not leave.'

By his standards this was clearly a major concession and there seemed very little point in pushing it—the man had about as much flexibility as a chunk of granite.

Her lashes lowered as her eyes slid downwards skimming his long, lean body. He was hard in a physical as well as intellectual sense, but, added the voice in her head, much warmer to the touch.

Before she could prevent it an image formed in Dervla's head of pale fingers trailing down the perfectly formed contours of his golden chest.

Utterly appalled at the intrusive image—for heaven's sake, she was a professional!—Dervla grunted some sort of acknowledgement and moved past him.

Once she began to work and focus her attention on what she was actually here to do it was a relief to be able to push all thought of warm, silky-textured skin from her mind. Heaven knew how it got there to begin with!

Dervla was pleased to discover the young Italian boy's observations gave no cause for concern. Casting a final expert eye over the boy's pale face, she smoothed back a hank of dark hair from his brow and murmured, 'All done for now, Alberto.'

Straightening up, she walked to the bottom of the bed and washed her hands with the gel provided before she acknowledged the father's presence.

'He's doing—'

'Let me guess, as well as can be expected. *Dio*, do you people ever run out of meaningless platitudes?'

'Your son is young and strong and the surgery went well, Mr Bruni. You really shouldn't anticipate problems before they happen,' she counselled calmly.

'You were talking to him?'

'Yes, I always explain what I'm doing to patients.'

He angled a dark brow and winced slightly as the movement evidently tugged at the raw open edges of the deep gash on his forehead. 'It does have a soothing quality.'

She stared at him with a perplexed frown.

'Your voice.' Before she could decide how to respond to this comment his attention shifted back to his son. 'If he had not gone back for that damned computer game…a computer game!' He closed his eyes and inhaled, rubbing the indentation between his brows as he rose to his feet.

He stood there towering over her, staring down at his son's bruised face, a nerve clenching in his angular jaw as he sucked in air through flared nostrils before adding in a harsh driven voice, 'My son might die because I wanted to teach him a lesson about values, that being a rich man's only child doesn't mean you don't have to work. He went back for his game because he knew I wouldn't replace something lost through his carelessness. That might prove to be an expensive lesson—for Alberto.'

Dervla watched, sympathy lodged like a stone in her chest, as his dark lashes swept downwards.

The Italian swallowed hard, causing a convulsive ripple

beneath the brown skin of his throat as he made a visible effort to suck in the emotions that spilled out.

Dervla tensed as his dark eyes lifted.

'What? No "It's not your fault, Mr Bruni"?' he drawled sarcastically.

'I'm sure you don't need me to tell you that,' she said quietly.

'You are clearly not a parent.'

Dervla flinched as if he had inadvertently touched an exposed nerve. 'No,' she agreed levelly. 'I am not a parent.' And never would be.

'A game worth a few pounds and I own the company…' The rest of his raw observations were delivered in a staccato burst of Italian, but the sentiment of self-loathing was pretty much the same in any language.

Dervla looked at his hands, clenched white-knuckled in frustration, and acted without thinking. She reached out and covered his hand with her own. 'It wasn't your fault,' she told him fiercely. 'It's the monsters that planned this atrocity. Nothing,' she added firmly, 'will be achieved from beating yourself up about it or imagining a hundred if-only scenarios.'

Gianfranco Bruni froze, his eyes glued to the small hand curled over his.

The irrelevant thought that he had rather lovely hands, shapely and strong with long tapering fingers, flashed through her head as she gave one last squeeze before releasing her grip.

'You really mustn't blame yourself,' she insisted earnestly.

There was a short uncomfortable pause.

'My son's welfare is all that need concern you, Nurse. I thought we had established I do not need my hand held or my brow mopped by a ministering angel!' He gave a sub-zero smile, raised one sable brow and added, 'Do you understand?'

The colour flew to her cheeks. The man was hurting, sure, but was there any need for him to be quite so unpleasant?

'I understand,' she said, keeping her voice level.

'Good,' he grunted, dragging the chair closer to the bed and folding his long length into it. 'I'm sure you graduated top of empathy in your class, but save it for someone who prefers mushy sentiment to proficiency.'

'I hope one doesn't preclude the other, Mr Bruni,' she said quietly.

'Dervla, is there a problem?'

Dervla, who hadn't been aware of the charge nurse's approach, started as he spoke. She took a deep breath and willed her pulse rate to slow. 'No, no problem.'

John gave a nod, but did not look entirely convinced as his glance slid from Dervla to the tall Italian. 'Mr Bruni, I've arranged for a porter with a wheelchair to take you to Casualty. One of the plastic surgeons is standing by.'

Gianfranco Bruni looked at him blankly.

'Porter?'

'With a chair.'

'You think I am an invalid?'

'It's hospital policy, Mr Bruni, and the sooner that head wound is sutured, the better.'

'My head?'

Dervla was not surprised to see John's expression sharpen into suspicious concern as he looked at Gianfranco Bruni. The Italian looked so baffled by the reference that she suspected he had forgotten he was injured, or maybe he hadn't even noticed.

'You've got a deep gash six inches long on your forehead,' the charge nurse explained. 'You didn't lose consciousness at any point, did you?'

Gianfranco Bruni gave a dismissive wave and turned away. 'It's a scratch,' he retorted irritably.

Dervla's exasperation got the better of her. 'Your scratch is bleeding all over the floor.'

The Italian's head slewed back. 'Who, Nurse, do you think you are talking to?'

'I think I'm talking to a man who would prefer deference to the truth, an extremely stubborn man who wouldn't relinquish control if his life depended on it.'

It was hard to tell which of the two men was looking more astonished by her outburst.

'Dervla,' John began, 'it might be better if you—'

'It's bleeding.' They both turned in unison to see Gianfranco Bruni looking at the blood on his fingers, his expression oddly blank.

'Don't be alarmed,' she cautioned, regarding him warily. He wasn't the most obvious candidate, but she had seen big, tough-looking chaps faint away at the sight of blood—especially their own.

His head came up with a snap. 'I am not alarmed. Just give me some tape—a dressing or something to cover it.'

'This is not a do-it-yourself hospital, Mr. Bruni,' John intervened quietly.

'She can do it,' the Italian said suddenly, stabbing a finger towards Dervla.

Dervla's jaw dropped. 'Me!' She really hoped he didn't mean what she thought he did.

'Nurse Smith is—'

'Is she not able?'

'Of course she's able, but after the plastic surgeon has sewn you up there will hardly be a scar.'

The Italian looked at the other man, his upper lip curling as he snarled contemptuously, 'You think I give a damn about my face?'

His hand lifted in an angry gesture that invited them to look at the object under discussion. It was an invitation that Dervla found hard to refuse.

He might dismiss his looks, but in her opinion a man who looked like him could be forgiven a little of the vanity he appeared to despise.

'Surely your surgeons have better things to do today than

sew up my scratch? My son is not the only one fighting for his life,' he bit through clenched teeth as he stared with dark pain-filled eyes at the unconscious figure in the bed. 'I want her,' he said without looking at Dervla. 'Nurse Smith.'

They said it was always good to be wanted—but they were wrong, Dervla decided grimly as her stomach churned with un-professional trepidation.

John shrugged, shot Dervla a questioning look and to her dismay asked, 'Are you all right with that, Dervla?'

Dervla, who was about as all right with it as putting her hand in a live electric socket, struggled to conceal her irrational horror.

'Don't worry. I am not litigious,' the Italian remarked as she hesitated.

Her head turned and her eyes brushed the cynical deepset eyes of the injured billionaire. 'I'm not worried about you suing me.' And she had no doubt about her ability to perform the relatively minor procedure; she had sutured hundreds of wounds. No, her reluctance had more to do with an irrational and strong disinclination to touch the man.

'The plastic surgeon would make a much better job. I don't usually—'

His broad shoulders lifted fractionally in a fluid shrug. 'So be flexible.'

'Because you won't be?'

The suggestion brought his narrowed scrutiny zeroing in on her face. Beside her Dervla was dimly aware of John looking astonished and not very happy.

'You worked that out faster than most people.'

Was that a compliment? she wondered. The lift of one corner of his wide, sensually sculpted mouth might have been his version of a smile…? But then again, she thought, maybe not.

It was five minutes later when Dervla led the way to the small curtained-off section very conscious of the tall man who followed her. She motioned him to the seat and angled the light

on his face before washing her hands and sliding them into
sterile gloves.

As she leaned closer to clean the wound her nostrils quivered
in response to the male scent of his body. The harsh artificial
light, not normally flattering, served to emphasise the hollows
and planes of his strong-boned face.

'I'm sorry.' Under the accumulated grime and blood there was
a grey tinge to his skin that she was guessing was not normal.

'For what?'

'Hurting you.'

'I think it's hurting you more than me.' The realisation
brought a flicker of amusement to his deepset eyes. 'Are you
sure you have the right temperament to be a nurse?'

'Not everyone,' she retorted tartly, 'thinks empathy is a bad
thing.' She paused, a swab in her hand, and asked hopefully,
'Are you sure that you wouldn't prefer one of the doctors to do
this? It really is a deep wound.'

'Just get on with it.'

'Fine, if that's what you want. I'll just put in some local an-
aesthetic to—'

He shook his dark head irritably. 'Forget that. Just sew the
damned thing up.'

'You really don't have to prove how macho you are. There's
nobody here but me.'

He looked at her with a contemptuous smile. 'I thought
you'd enjoy having me at your mercy,' he taunted.

Like most nurses Dervla had ducked more than one blow
from drunks in Casualty, and on one memorable occasion had
had her shoulder dislocated by a confused patient who had
wanted to jump out a second-floor window, but none had made
her feel quite as vulnerable or as angry as this man did.

Dervla, who had always prided herself on her professionalism,
was deeply dismayed. In her job you simply couldn't mix professional with personal—it was a line you simply did not cross.

Of course she was only human and inevitably she felt a personal connection with some patients that she did not with others.

With this man she wouldn't want a connection of any variety!

'Fine.'

She worked as swiftly as she could, her tongue caught between her teeth as she concentrated on knitting the torn flesh neatly together. He didn't flinch, which could mean she was really good at what she was doing, but more likely meant he was too stupidly stubborn to admit it hurt.

'There,' she said, taking a step back to view her handiwork. 'You're done. Now take things slowly—you might feel…'

Before she had finished speaking he had removed the sterile towel she had placed around his shoulders and was on his feet.

He stood, drew back the curtain and arched an enquiring brow at her.

'I might feel what, Nurse?'

'Faint if you get up too quickly.'

For a moment his teeth flashed white, his lean bronzed face making him look momentarily a lot younger, and—had it not been clearly impossible—even more attractive. 'Sorry to disappoint you.'

A wet coat being slung onto the sofa beside her jerked Dervla abruptly back to the present. She blinked from the images on the television screen to the figure who was heading to the kitchen where the sounds proclaimed she was filling a kettle.

Sue returned a moment later. 'It's absolutely foul out there,' she complained, running her hands through her wet dark curls. 'You've been crying!' she accused, peering at Dervla's damp face.

'No…' Dervla lifted a hand to her face and felt the salty moisture on her skin. 'I suppose I might have,' she admitted.

'This,' her friend said, kicking off her shoes quite literally—they hit the opposite wall, 'is driving me crazy. I've respected your privacy but I'm only human. I have to know—why did you walk out on the delicious Gianfranco? Who clearly adores the ground you walk on.' She flopped down on the sofa beside Dervla and pushed her coat on the floor. 'So spill. Give me all the lurid details.'

'He doesn't adore me or the ground I walk on.' The only thing Gianfranco adored was his son and the memory of his dead wife. Dervla raised her empty mug. 'To new beginnings!'

'What?' Sue said, staring at her friend's bitter face with concern.

'That was the toast Carla gave when she took me to lunch that first week. She said it was marvellous that Gianfranco had met me, that he was finally able to move on and have a relationship without feeling he was being unfaithful to Sara's memory.'

'Well, I'd prefer the woman if she had the odd skin blemish, but she's got a point, Dervla—'

'Only she was wrong,' Dervla cut in huskily. 'He hadn't moved on—he hasn't, and he doesn't love me.'

'Don't be stupid. Of course—'

'No.' Dervla shook her head slowly from side to side. 'He never pretended to, he still loves her.' My life isn't over, she reminded herself. It just feels that way. 'It's not a baby he doesn't want—it's my baby.'

Sue stared at her with eyes like saucers. 'Baby! But I thought that you couldn't have a baby. You thought it would be the deal-breaker when you told him,' she reminded her friend. 'You were over the moon when he said it was no problem with him.'

Dervla nodded miserably. 'He said he already had Alberto and he didn't want any more children. That we had a ready-made family.'

'But you want your own, and there's a chance…?'

Dervla nodded. Sue was one of the few people she had ever told about the tragic long-term consequences of complications after a perforated appendix and the subsequent peritonitis that had put her on the critical list in her teens.

'I might be able to have a baby, but not,' she added, the tears beginning to overflow in earnest from her tragic emerald eyes, 'with Gianfranco. I have to choose a baby or him.'

Sue's arms went around her as she began to weep loudly.

CHAPTER FIVE

'WELL, what do you think?' the man at the head of the table asked, lifting his dark head from the spreadsheet he had been studying.

There was a silence in the room as he allowed his hooded gaze to rest on each face in turn. He could read panic in several faces as the executives frantically tried to decide what he wanted to hear.

Gianfranco felt a flash of irritation—he did not surround himself with yes-men or -women.

'Does nobody have an opinion?' *Or a backbone?*

It seemed that nobody had, or if they did they were unwilling to express it. Gianfranco felt his frustration escalate in the growing silence.

'Perhaps there is somewhere else you want to be?' he suggested with silken sarcasm.

The trouble, he mused, with people was they couldn't separate their personal life from their professional life. It was a fatal mistake and one that he couldn't understand. He had always compartmentalised his life, it was simply a matter of discipline.

His lashes lowered as his dark glance brushed the metal-banded watch on his wrist. He wondered if his assistant, who seemed less than her usual efficient self today, had remembered to relay the message to everyone concerned that he wanted all personal calls to be immediately diverted in here.

The sound of a phone ringing broke the lengthening silence. Gianfranco began to count, his hands clenched into white-knuckled fists as he resisted the urge to immediately pull it from his jacket pocket.

Nobody else reached to check if the call was for them. Gianfranco Bruni's dislike of such interruptions was well known and nobody would have dreamt of not switching off their mobiles before going into a meeting chaired by him.

It was Gianfranco himself who, after the second ring, pulled a phone from the breast pocket of his jacket and, after glancing at it, rose abruptly, excusing himself.

'The wife,' the only woman present at the high-powered meeting predicted, unwittingly echoing Gianfranco's first thought when he had heard the ring.

No one disagreed.

Before his marriage the previous year Gianfranco would not have disregarded his own rule concerning interruptions. Since the wedding to which no one, least of all media cameras, had been invited there had been some significant changes. It was rumoured that Gianfranco even took a day off occasionally, but that was only a rumour.

'Well, I hope she says something to put him in a less vile mood.'

'Yes, our leader is not his usual sunny self this afternoon, is he?' someone agreed drily.

There was a generous noise of assent around the table.

'Have you met her? The wife, that is?' one of the executives asked curiously.

The gentle chatter around the table stopped and a couple of people nodded to confirm they had.

One said, 'My mother got me to take her to the opening

of the new children's hospice. It turns out to be his wife's brainchild.'

'I suppose even a lady who lunches needs something to put on her CV.'

'That's what I thought, but it turns out she's really hands-on. Literally actually,' he recalled with a reminiscent smile. 'She was down on her hands and knees rolling around on the grass barefoot with some of the kids.'

'She doesn't sound like a Gianfranco Bruni girlfriend.'

'She's not—she's his wife. Maybe that's the difference. You're not wrong, though. She really isn't his usual type.'

'Presumably not hard on the eye, though?'

'She's pretty,' the speaker agreed. 'A redhead, green eyes, freckles.' He gave a reminiscent smile. 'Really great, sexy laugh.'

'Sounds like Ricardo was smitten,' someone said slyly, and there was laughter as the middle-aged man in question flushed but didn't deny the charge.

'I've never even seen a photo of her.'

Another result of his sudden marriage had been that Gianfranco, who had once supplied the gossip columns with acres of copy, had pretty much slipped off the photo-opportunity map and retreated behind the sort of security that people who were as rich as he was could.

'Not exactly a party girl, then, the redhead?'

'She is English, though?' The person who asked the question glanced at the closed door before he spoke. Being caught gossiping about the boss would do his promotion prospects no good at all.

'I'm not sure. Her name doesn't sound English…Der something…?'

'Dervla.' It was the sole female who supplied the bride's name.

'Wasn't she a model?'

'Doubt it. She's not tall enough,' one person who had met her said.

'Well, from what I've heard…'

The men leaned forward to catch the woman's words as her voice dropped to a confidential hiss. 'I don't know how true it is, you understand, but my friend's cousin—he works at the hospital in London where she was apparently working when they met.'

'She's a doctor?'

'No, a nurse…she looked after his son when they were caught up in that terrorist thing.'

There were murmurs as the people present recalled the horrific incident she spoke of.

'I think it's *so* romantic,' she added dreamily.

One of the men, the youngest there, who had been struggling to defend a business decision earlier to his critical boss, laughed and said scornfully, 'Gianfranco Bruni doesn't have a romantic bone in his body. A couple of years' time and he'll probably trade her in for a new model.'

When Gianfranco had reached for his phone and not seen Dervla's name he had needed to dig deep into his seriously depleted reserves of self-control to maintain a semblance of composure.

At least until he was out of the room.

In the corridor he gritted his teeth and ground one clenched fist into the other. It had been forty-eight hours and not a word—not one word!

For all he knew she could be lying unconscious in a hospital bed. Fighting against the swell of crushing anxiety in his chest, he pushed his fingers deep into the ebony hair that sprang from his temples and inhaled deeply, forcing the air into his lungs before expelling it in a gusty sigh.

Get a grip, man, he counselled himself as he smoothed back the tousled hair from his brow and adjusted his tie.

Damn the woman!

'Gianfranco!'

Gianfranco turned his head at the sound of the familiar voice and forced his lips into a semblance of a smile. *Normally* he would have been genuinely pleased to see Angelo Martinos, who had been his closest friend since the days when they both shared the distinction of being the only 'foreigners' at the English prep school they had been sent to at the ages of nine and ten respectively.

'Angelo, what brings you here?' he asked without enthusiasm.

'Called on the off chance. They told me you were in a meeting.' He raised an interrogative brow as he scanned his friend's face. 'Not a good one, apparently…?'

Now *this* was one of the reasons why Angelo was the last person to see right now. It wasn't easy to pull the wool over his eyes, and he thought being his best friend gave him the right to pry.

'You know how it is,' he returned, doubting that his happily married friend knew the first thing about being put through an emotional meat-grinder by his wife.

Angelo's wife apparently thought that his every word was a pearl of wisdom, whereas Gianfranco's own bride never lost an opportunity to challenge him.

'Feel like a coffee?' Angelo wondered, his glance lingering briefly on the razor cut on Gianfranco's angular jaw. When a moment later he noticed the mismatched socks his eyebrows hit his hairline—impeccable and effortless elegance were descriptions frequently ascribed to his friend.

Gathering his straying attention and wishing his friend would take the hint and go, Gianfranco shook his head and said, 'Not really,' in a discouraging way that would have made ninety-nine people out of a hundred back off, but not Angelo.

'I'm at a loose end. Kate and her mum are baby shopping. I was getting in the way.'

'Sorry, I'm pretty snowed under today. I just ducked out to take a call from Alberto. I should ring back.'

'I hardly recognised Alberto when I saw him. Thirteen and

he must be nearly six feet. At this rate you'll be looking up at him before long.'

'Maybe,' said Gianfranco, who at six five rarely had to look up at anyone.

'I don't envy him puberty. It was hell.'

Gianfranco choked off a bitter laugh. 'For you? I don't think so, unless adolescent hell involved every girl you wanted and—'

'I only got them because you knocked them back, Gianfranco,' Angelo, ever the pragmatist, cut in. 'Your problem, my friend, was you put women on a pedestal.'

Gianfranco had been approaching his twentieth birthday when he thought he had found one who belonged on that pedestal. By the time he realised that beyond the perfect face the innocent-eyed woman he had woven his romantic fantasies around—a barmaid who worked in the local hotel—had actually been not so innocent and rather more interested in his sexual stamina than his philosophical reflections and pathetic poetry, it had been too late.

She had been pregnant and to his family's horror he had married her and become a father at twenty.

'I was intense.' Gianfranco cringed now to think of the boy he had been. 'And an idiot.'

'You were a romantic,' Angelo retorted indulgently. 'And I was shallow, but now we are both older and wiser, not to mention happily married, men. It was a great weekend, which is what brings me here. We'd love to return your hospitality. Kate wants to know if you're both free on the eighteenth, always supposing nothing has happened on the baby front…?'

'Eighteenth…I probably, yes…no…I'm not sure.'

Angelo's scrutiny sharpened as he stared at his friend. In the twenty-five years he had known him, Gianfranco had never to his knowledge been *not sure* about anything.

'Well, when you are just get Dervla to give Kate a ring. And how is Dervla?' Angelo asked casually.

Gianfranco met his friend's eyes and lied unblinkingly. 'She's fine.'

Well, it wasn't actually a lie. She might well be fine. She might be totally fine after walking out on her husband. Gianfranco's sense of outrage and the throbbing in his temple swelled in unison as an image of her standing at the front door of their home flashed into his head.

'You're being ridiculous, Dervla.'

She stuck out her chin and glared at him through tear-misted eyes, emerald eyes, so intensely green when they'd first met he had assumed she was wearing contact lenses, shimmering.

'There's no need to work yourself up, Gianfranco. After all, it doesn't really matter what I do.'

'What are you talking about?'

'Well, I'm not important. I'm just a temporary someone who's passing through, someone who isn't good enough to take responsibility for your son…and don't give me that guff about our ready-made family because you shut me out totally. Bottom line is I'm good enough to have sex with but not good enough to be the mother of your child!'

'That's totally ludicrous. There's nothing temporary about our marriage.'

Eyes narrowed, she lifted her chin in challenge. 'So you want a baby?'

He ground his teeth and reminded her, 'You were the one that said that you didn't need children to have a fulfilling life.'

She glared at him with withering scorn. 'That, you stupid man, was when I thought I couldn't have any!'

'You knew when we married that I did not want children. I haven't changed.'

'That's the problem!'

'Don't play cryptic word games with me, Dervla.'

'I'm not playing anything any more. I'm leaving.'

He could see her slim back shaking as she fumbled opening

the big oak-banded door. He focused on his anger to stop himself taking her in his arms to wipe away the tears he knew were pouring down her cheeks. He walked up behind her and put his hand on her shoulder.

'I admit you have a flare for drama, but this is enough, Dervla.'

She didn't turn around, just whispered, 'Goodbye, Gianfranco.' And walked through the door.

And he stood there watching, never quite believing that she would go…expecting her to run back through the door at any moment admitting that she had been totally in the wrong.

But there had been no running and no Dervla.

She had left him and their home. The home she had put her indelible mark on. Gianfranco pushed aside the disturbing thought that the mark she had put on him was much more indelible.

Having learnt the hard way that romantic love was a sham, a form of self-hypnosis, Gianfranco had never expected to marry again.

The fact was he had married because the woman he'd wanted would not accept less.

And you tried so hard to persuade her otherwise…?

Gianfranco's eyebrows twitched into an irritated frown at the mental interruption. His decision to marry had not been based on anything as unreliable as emotions. Like all the decisions he made, he had weighed the pros and cons and come to the conclusion that marriage was something he could live with.

And Dervla was something he did not wish to live without— at least for the moment—though he did not doubt that the overwhelming compulsion he had to bind her to him would fade.

The intensity of it had shaken him, but he did not read any magical significance into it. Feelings of that sort of intensity were not durable; they did not signify a meeting of soul mates. The problems began when you started to believe they did.

He had not changed his opinion of marriage. He still pitied the fools entering into it with a lot of unrealistic phoney, sentimental expectations.

The trouble was people forgot that basically marriage was a legal contract. He had every intention of fulfilling his end of that contract, a contract that could be dissolved if the balance of those pros and cons shifted.

Marriage was like Christmas—people expected too much and were inevitably disappointed.

His expectation had been more realistic the second time around—but he didn't think it was realistic to expect your wife to change the rules a year in. It wasn't as if they had not discussed the subject—he had never even imagined she felt that way.

Not strictly true, said the voice in his head as an incident he had mentally filed as insignificant popped unbidden into his head. He had been giving her the grand tour of her new home at this time.

'This was my nursery… I thought you could use it as a study. The view is really magnificent.'

He pretended not to see the pain and hopeless longing in her face as she touched the carved wood of the antique crib in the corner. Guilt gnawed at him, he hadn't wanted to see it.

'A study would be nice,' she agreed quietly.

'Of course, you can redecorate just as you please. I've got the names of some very good interior designers.'

'What would I want with an interior designer?' she asked, shaking back her tawny curls.

Gianfranco was relieved to see no trace of the previous sadness in her eyes as she looked up at him with that half-quizzical teasing look of hers.

'An interior designer isn't going to live here, silly, we are. A home should evolve…' she explained earnestly. 'Be filled with memories.'

Gianfranco was pretty sure that by memories she had meant some of the curious and totally valueless objects she took pleasure in discovering and producing for his admiration, and not the memories that were causing him torture of an unbearable kind.

At the time making love to his wife in every room of their large and many-roomed home had seemed an excellent idea, but now that good idea had come back to haunt him. Quite literally! He couldn't walk into a room without being assaulted by sweet erotic recollections.

'We thought she seemed a little…*quiet*…?'

Gianfranco shook his head to free himself from the images playing in it. He dragged his eyes up from the floor, where presumably he had been staring like some catatonic moron, until his friend's face came into frame.

He gave a careless shrug and ignored the question in his friend's eyes.

If he had been going to confide in anyone it would have been Angelo, but it was not his way to offload his problems on others.

'She was a little tired.'

Angelo grinned. 'Nine months ago Kate had some similar symptoms.'

Gianfranco's jaw clenched. 'Dervla is not pregnant.'

Angelo stepped into the lift, his expression openly speculative. 'Sorry, my mind is a bit one-track at the moment.'

Gianfranco unclenched his fists and struggled to respond appropriately to the social cue. 'How is Kate?'

'Fine. Give Dervla our love, Gianfranco, and I hope she's feeling less…tired soon.'

Gianfranco nodded absently, thinking that this message would take lower priority than many things he needed to say to his wife when he saw her.

He was mentally polishing the more personal messages as he walked into the office and dialled his son's number. As he was not fully concentrating on what Alberto said he assumed initially he had misheard him.

'What did you say, Alberto?'

'I said I'm running away.'

CHAPTER SIX

OF COURSE you are.

Gianfranco dragged a hand through his hair and glanced at his reflection in the mirrored surface of a wall cabinet. Despite the concerted efforts of his nearest and dearest there were no white streaks in the hair of the man who looked back at him.

But it could only be a matter of time.

'I'm assuming this is some kind of joke?'

It seemed a safe assumption. Having broken family tradition, he had sent his son to a day school in Florence. Alberto was on a school field trip to Brussels to see the European Parliament in action, safely supervised by teachers.

'I'm in Calais at the moment, but the ferry leaves in a few minutes.'

Staring out of the window at the traffic below, he shook his head, still feeling slightly more irritation than concern. 'You're in Brussels.'

'No, Calais.'

Gianfranco felt the concern versus irritation dip towards concern.

'Calais?'

'I told you—I've run away.'

Gianfranco's stomach muscles clenched in icy dread as he

realised this was no warped teenage sense of humour he was dealing with, but a genuine situation.

'You are actually in Calais…?' Gianfranco struggled to get his head around it.

How could a thirteen-year-old schoolboy meant to be in Brussels in the care of teachers be in Calais?

Thoughts of abduction and kidnap flashed into his head to be almost immediately dismissed. Alberto's voice was not that of a scared victim. Like someone coming out of a trance, he dragged a hand down his jaw and exhaled.

'You've run away? From me?' Why not? It was becoming quite a fashionable thing to do. If this was true Alberto wouldn't be sounding so chirpy once he got his hands on him, Gianfranco decided grimly.

'Yes, I just said so, didn't I? So if the school contacts you tell them I'm fine. They might have noticed I'm missing by now.'

'Might have noticed!' Gianfranco choked. He pushed aside the thought of what he would say to the teachers who had failed so miserably in their duty. There were more important things to think about. 'How did you get to Calais? Are you alone?'

'I hitched.'

His teenage son's explanation made Gianfranco's blood run cold. 'You hitched a lift?'

Impervious to the horror in his father's voice, the teenager added tetchily, 'You're not usually this slow, Dad. I know what you're thinking but the lorry driver was a really nice guy, not a pervert or anything. I told him I was seventeen and he believed me.'

Gianfranco bit back a curse and rolled his eyes heavenwards. He was having a nightmare, that was the only explanation, he decided.

Every parent knew it was a delicate line—the one between wrapping your children up in cotton wool and letting them run around oblivious to the dangers that lurked for the unsuspecting.

Like every other parent he wanted to keep his child safe. He had always been conscious that there was also a danger that an overprotective parent could stifle any sense of adventure in a child. In his efforts not to quash the spirit of adventure in his son he might, Gianfranco acknowledged grimly, have gone a little too far the other way.

'Listen to me very carefully,' Gianfranco said slowly.

'I can't. My battery's low and, don't worry, I can look after myself, you know, Dad.'

'Would it be pushy of me to ask why you're running away?'

'You might be divorcing Dervla, but I'm not.'

'Divorce!' Gianfranco yelled down the line. 'There will be no divorce.'

'That was my eardrum you just perforated. And if anyone asks I'll tell them I'd prefer to live with her.'

'Thank you very much,' Gianfranco inserted drily in response to this warning. 'Let me remind you again, nobody has mentioned divorce.' And nobody will.

'Not yet,' his son said darkly. 'But it doesn't take a genius to see where things were heading left to you two. So I decided you needed some help.'

'This form of *help* involves you running away?' Gianfranco tried to control his temper as he made a rapid mental calculation of how soon he could get to England before his son got into any more trouble.

'But where, or rather *who*, am I running to? I mean as a responsible parent you have to come get me, it's totally legit and there's no question of you chasing after her. I reckon you'll be all over each other about twenty seconds after you see each other.'

Not many things shocked Gianfranco to silence, but this nonchalant prediction did.

I'm being manipulated by a thirteen-year-old. A reluctant laugh was torn from his throat. If he's like this now, what will he be like by the time he's eighteen?

Hearing the laugh, the boy gave a sigh of relief. 'I knew you'd like my plan. Cool or what? Which reminds me, Dad, would you ring Dervla and ask her to pick me up at the ferry terminal? I think the boat gets in around six. Look, my battery really is low. I'll be in touch later…'

The line went dead and after a short pause Gianfranco keyed in a number.

Dervla took another doughnut from the bag that Sue had dumped on the tea tray. 'I don't usually like these,' she said, taking a large bite.

'You need a sugar hit. Trust me, I'm a nurse,' Sue said, helping herself. 'Look, Dervla, I think things have just got out of proportion. You two are meant to be together. Give him time and I guarantee he'll come around about the baby thing. He loves you.'

'You're totally wrong. Gianfranco doesn't love me. He never pretended to be in love with me, not even when he proposed,' she admitted in a voice that cracked with emotion.

In fact he had made it pretty clear that romantic love was an encumbrance that had no place in his life.

Sue looked sympathetic but unsurprised. 'Some men find it hard to articulate their feelings.'

Dervla's eyelashes swept upwards. Her green eyes were bleak as she gave an odd little laugh. 'Not Gianfranco,' she promised.

Gianfranco could be very articulate, especially when it came to exposing romantic love for the sham he believed it was. His feelings on the subject were clear and Gianfranco had no problem when it came to clarity.

Clarity was his thing, she reflected bitterly. Her husband was not a man for whom grey areas existed.

'He just doesn't have the feelings to express…not for me, at least,' she added bleakly.

Dervla had suspected early on that it wasn't love that Gianfranco didn't believe in, it was the possibility of him ever finding the love he had shared with his first wife, the love of his life, with anyone else.

Being a woman in love, she had ignored the deafening warning bells and decided she would be the one to teach him he could love again.

Feeling the frustrated resentment building inside her, she defiantly reached for another doughnut. It would serve Gianfranco—who had likened her to a sleek and supple little cat—right if she gained twenty pounds! She was definitely beginning to see the attraction of comfort eating.

'He told me when he proposed that he wasn't in love with me.'

The older girl shook her head in disbelief. 'And I thought Italian men were meant to be romantic,' she exclaimed, looking disillusioned.

'He still loves Alberto's mother. She was beautiful and perfect and—'

'I hate to point out the obvious, but this paragon is also no longer with us, Dervla.'

Dervla's mouth twisted into a bitter smile. 'Have you ever tried competing with a ghost?'

Sue's expression softened with sympathy. 'Is that how you felt?'

'She was beautiful.'

'So are you!' Sue protested.

Dervla gave an exasperated shake of her head. 'Not pretty—beautiful.'

'Does he mention her a lot?'

Dervla gave a sniff and shook her head. 'Never. See,' she said when she saw Sue's expression. 'You think that's a bad sign too.'

'Not necessarily.'

'Carla says he finds it too painful. She says Sara was his soul mate, they never argued and she—'

'I get the picture,' Sue intervened quickly. 'The man has baggage and a son.' She chewed worriedly on her lower lip as she studied her friend's unhappy, downcast features. 'God, Dervla, did you have to marry him? Couldn't you have just had sex?'

'That's what he said.'

Sue's eyes went saucer-wide. 'And you said…?'

'Obviously we'd already—' Dervla broke off, blushing, and Sue repressed a grin. 'He made this ridiculously big thing of me being a virgin at twenty-six.'

'You were a virgin!'

Sue's astonished exclamation brought Dervla's head up with a jerk.

'Gianfranco was your first lover?'

Dervla bit her lip and nodded.

'Wow!'

They both reached in unison for another doughnut as the phone began to ring.

Sue moved towards it and Dervla cried out urgently, 'No, leave it!'

Her friend shrugged and settled back in her seat.

Teeth clenched, Dervla stood ten more seconds before she broke and picked it up.

'Hello.'

'Dervla.'

His deep honey-timbred drawl was more frayed around the edges than normal but Dervla would have been able to distinguish it in the middle of a male voice choir.

Her mind went blank.

'Is that you or a heavy breather?'

She expelled the air trapped in her lungs in one gusty sigh and wiped her wet palm against her thigh.

'Hello, Gianfranco, how are you?' How are you? Why stop there, Dervla? Why not sound like a complete moron and ask him how the weather is there?

'How do you think I am, *cara*?'

She winced at the acid in his biting response and felt her

anger and resentment stir. As if he were the only one suffering here; as if she hadn't spent two days of hell.

'How would I know? Silence is kind of hard to interpret. I couldn't even read between the lines, because there weren't any. I'm actually feeling fairly honoured that you spared a moment to pick up the phone.'

There was a protracted silence that was more than adequate for Dervla to regret her hasty comments.

'So you missed me, then.'

He sounded so smug that if there hadn't been several hundred miles separating them she'd have hit him. Acknowledgement of the distance between them drew a desolate little sigh from her. How could you feel lonely in a place that until recently you had called home? But she did, her home was not here any longer, it was wherever Gianfranco was.

'Actually I've been too busy to miss you. There's been no time. I've been shopping and to lunch, catching up on old friends. We're on out way our now, actually. You only just caught me.'

At the other end of the phone Gianfranco snapped the pencil he was threading between his long fingers in two. 'So should I expect to see photos of you staggering out of nightclubs to appear in the tabloids?' he wondered in a sub-zero tone.

'Don't be absurd!' she snapped, conscious that nothing he said could be as absurd as her trying to convince anyone she didn't miss him.

God, the ache for him went bone deep.

'Well, if you could spare a moment out of your busy social diary…?'

Dervla nibbled on the sensitive flesh of her full lower lip. If he'd rung to say come back what was she going to do? Of course, he might have rung to say let's call it a day. The second possibility almost tipped her over the edge into total panic.

'If you've got something to say, Gianfranco, just say it.' Whatever he said, she told herself she could deal with it.

'We have a problem, Dervla.'

She closed her eyes, sure she knew what was coming: it was the second possibility. He was going to say let's call it a day—this relationship is more trouble than it's worth.

She had always wondered what she'd feel like when this happened. Now she knew—she wasn't going to feel anything at all.

She was numb.

'Well, it could be worse—you could have sent me an email.' Perhaps one day you'd be able to legally end a marriage that way, neat and clinically without any need for even looking at your partner.

Anger swelled inside her. She wanted to see Gianfranco. She wanted to tell him to his face what he was throwing away. She wanted to tell him that he was damned lucky she loved him and it was his loss.

Her chest tightened… Oh God, and mine, she thought, thinking of her life stretching ahead, a life of days when she would not hear Gianfranco's voice or see his face.

'Email? What are you talking about? No, don't tell me, there's no time. It's Alberto.'

'Alberto?' she echoed. 'Not a divorce?'

'Divorce?' A volley of Italian words they didn't teach in the polite surroundings of her language class came down the line. 'Have you been talking to Alberto?'

'No,' she said, turning her back on a wildly gesticulating Sue so that she could concentrate on what he was saying.

'Alberto has run away.'

It took several moments for the blunt statement to penetrate. When it did the blood drained from Dervla's face. She swayed.

'Oh, my God, no, is he…? How long? The police…' She sank into the chair that Sue placed behind her knees and whispered, 'I feel sick.'

Sue took the phone from her limp grasp and with a marshal light in her eyes waded right in.

'What the hell have you said to her? No, she damned well isn't all right!'

'I'm fine, Sue, will you give me—?'

'You're not fine,' Sue contradicted. 'She nearly passed out, you blithering idiot.'

Dervla, struggling to contain her nausea, groaned; with the best intentions in the world Sue was making matters worse. She could just imagine how Gianfranco would react under normal circumstances to being called a blithering idiot, but these were not normal circumstances—his son was missing.

If anything happened to Alberto she could not bear to think of how Gianfranco would react. He adored the boy. So did she.

I should be there with him.

Consumed with guilt that she wasn't there when he needed her most, Dervla got unsteadily to her feet. This was not a moment for wimpy fainting.

The next blistering instalment of Sue's indictment came to an abrupt halt as she said, 'Oh, God, I'm sorry. When… how…?' And began to listen.

'He's all right, Dervla. He rang his dad from Calais.'

With a gasp of relief Dervla snatched the phone from her friend's hand. 'Is it true? Alberto is safe?'

'He's fine, *cara*, though he won't be when I get my hands on him.' This grim observation drew a weak laugh from Dervla. 'He took a slight detour from the school excursion and ended up in Calais. You've got to admit the boy has ingenuity. He rang from the ferry. Apparently he's on the way to England.'

'Here! Well, at least you know he's safe. I wonder what on earth made him do something like that?' she puzzled. Alberto was about the most unmixed-up adolescent she had ever met. He was a total stranger to teenage angst. 'It's just so unlike him.'

'Who knows why a teenager does anything?'

Something in Gianfranco's voice made her wonder if he knew something that he wasn't telling her. It hurt that he was excluding her again.

'Can I do anything?'

'Yes, that's why I rang.'

Not because you needed to hear my voice. For a moment she longed with every fibre of her being for Gianfranco to want and need her as much as she did him. She wanted him to feel the same aching emptiness she did at this moment. She wanted him to love her.

Then on the heels of the thought came guilt. What a selfish, self-centred cow I am, she thought in disgust. Gianfranco was already feeling as bad as he could. His son was out there alone and, no matter how mature he seemed, Alberto was still a child and he was the only part Gianfranco had left of the woman he had loved—so Gianfranco already knew about the aching emptiness.

'Anything.' The word emerged with far more force than she had intended.

'That's a rash offer.'

'It's a genuine offer, Gianfranco. I love Alberto too, you know.'

'I know. He speaks very highly of you too.' This time she was sure the edge in Gianfranco's voice was unmistakable.

'Try not to worry,' she said, because she couldn't think of anything else to say that wasn't 'I love you'.

'I'm sending Eduardo over with the car. He'll be there in about half an hour. If you could meet Alberto off the ferry and take him back to the house?'

'Yes, of course.'

'I'll be there as soon as I can.'

'Fine, I'll see you then,' she said, trying to match his businesslike tone and, she suspected, failing pretty comprehensively.

She put the phone down and turned to Sue. 'You got the gist of that?'

Sue nodded. 'You're riding shotgun on the kid until Dad gets here.'

Dervla nodded.

'And after that?'

'After that, I suppose…' Dervla's slender shoulders lifted. 'I don't really know,' she admitted. 'He'll be here in about half an hour. I suppose I'd better get my things together.'

'I put your holdall in my bedroom.'

'Thanks.' Sue followed her into the bedroom and watched while she unzipped the bag to check the contents.

'So you're not coming back, then?'

'I suppose that depends.'

'On whether you choose Gianfranco or a baby?'

Hearing it put so bluntly made Dervla blanch.

'You know, I never even knew you wanted a baby. I thought you were totally all right with the situation.'

'I was, or at least I thought I was,' she amended huskily. 'Maybe,' she speculated, pushing her hair from her face with the crook of one elbow as she bent forward to pick up her toiletries from the floor, 'I'd just never met a man whose children I wanted to have.'

'You really love him, don't you?'

Dervla gave a laugh, pulled a scarf from her bag and, bunching her hair at the base of her neck, wound it around to secure it there. 'He's the only one who doesn't seem to realise I do, which, considering he's supposed to have a mind like a steel trap, is kind of ironic.'

'You could tell him?'

Dervla turned and angled her helpful friend an incredulous look. 'It's the last thing he wants to hear.'

'Maybe he should hear it. What are you going to do about the fertility treatment?'

'I suppose I'll just have to forget it.'

'Can you?'

Dervla's face creased with anguish as she admitted, 'It won't be easy. It was much easier to accept never having a child of my own while I knew there was no hope, but now...' Dervla stopped, unable to continue as her voice became totally suspended by tears.

Her visit to the fertility specialist had opened up all sorts of possibilities she hadn't let herself think about before.

Before Gianfranco had entered her life she had genuinely believed that she had accepted her infertility. There were, after all, other things in life than children.

It didn't make her any less of a woman.

Or did it, in Gianfranco's eyes at least?

She had never been able to push the question from her mind. He was such a terrific father to Alberto it seemed impossible to her that he wouldn't want other children and a woman who could provide those children.

As it turned out her fears had been totally unfounded. Gianfranco didn't want her babies.

'The chances of me conceiving naturally are virtually zero. Or "entering miracle territory", to quote the fertility specialist I saw.'

'*You've* already been to see a specialist?'

Dervla could understand her friend's surprise. It was a bit of a turn-about for someone who had always said she couldn't understand women who put themselves through repeated courses of IVF when statistically the chances of conceiving were so low.

'I know I said there was no way I'd put myself through that sort of thing, but at the time it wasn't a viable option for me. If you can't have something it makes life easier if you tell yourself you don't really want it.

'The doctor was cautiously optimistic, but this is a new technique and they're looking for suitable patients to be involved in a clinical trial. The chances are it wouldn't have worked anyway,' she said, zipping the bag and hefting it onto her shoulder.

Was she going to allow her reluctance to let go of that faint possibility kill her marriage stone-dead?

'Marriage is about compromise,' she said, as much for her own benefit as Sue's. Halfway to the door she stopped and turned, her eyes filled with tears she refused to allow to fall.

'You know, every time I feel like I'm getting close he pushes me away. He doesn't care for me the way I—' She stopped abruptly. Regretting and deeply embarrassed by the impulsive confidence the moment it left her lips, Dervla lifted her chin to a determined angle and smiled mechanically as her eyes slid from Sue's. 'I'd better go downstairs and wait for Eduardo.'

She was on the stairs when Sue's voice drifted down the stairwell echoing against the concrete walls.

'Maybe he cares too much, Dervla, and it scares him. Just a thought…'

Sue meant well, but she didn't know Gianfranco; he wasn't scared of anything.

The limousine was waiting for her. The chauffeur jumped out when he saw her and took her bag, enquiring politely after her health.

Dervla slid into the back with a murmured, 'Hello, Eduardo.'

As the engine purred to life she was unable to prevent her thoughts returning to the first time she had travelled in this car. It had been a day for firsts: her first trip in a limo and her first time with a man.

Neither had been planned. She had not woken up that day and thought, Hey, this would be a good day to lose my virginity. Who can I think of to oblige? And if he owns a limo that would be a 'two birds with one stone' scenario.

CHAPTER SEVEN

ACTUALLY that day had started out a bit of a stinker. One of Dervla's patients, a dear old man who had fought his way back to health after heart surgery, had passed away quite suddenly.

Not inclined to linger and chat in the changing rooms, she had hurried hoping to catch the earlier bus home. As she'd walked through the swing doors of the main entrance she had paused to pull up the hood of her jacket against the rain.

Peering up at the grey sky had not improved her mood. She had been preparing to make the dash across the busy road to the bus stop when she'd felt a hand on her shoulder.

She had turned and found her eyes on a level with the middle button of an expensive leather jacket. She had known that underneath the jacket the owner wore a pale grey cashmere sweater.

She had tilted her head and just managed to keep the inappropriate—almost as inappropriate as wondering about what he'd look like minus the cashmere—gasp locked in her throat. As her eyes had connected with his dramatically dark eyes the weariness that had made her steps leaden had been instantly swept away in the wake of an adrenaline rush.

At least she had hoped it was adrenaline, but if her hormones had been involved she would have been in trouble because she had forgotten how to breathe. It might have helped if he'd moved his hand, but it had still been on her shoulder and he'd been showing no inclination to move it any time soon.

Breathing unevenly, but breathing, which was a relief, she had sketched a smile.

For the past week she had seen Gianfranco Bruni every day. Dervla had been able to observe first hand the satisfactory healing of the wound she had sutured. She had also been able to observe his devotion to his son and his ability to function with very little sleep.

He had sat at his son's bedside for thirty-six hours straight before finally leaving it for long enough to shower, change his clothes and return clean-shaven. Dishevelled and bloodstained he had looked more good-looking than any man had a right to—scrubbed up he had been simply off-the-scale gorgeous!

Once news of his presence had spread people had started appearing from all over the hospital on the limpest of pretexts until John had let it be known that his unit was not a zoo, and anyone there without a valid reason would have some explaining to do.

Despite the fact Gianfranco's absences had only ever been brief he had still oozed a restless vitality. You got the impression that if invited to scale the odd mountain before supper he'd leap at the chance.

More than once as Dervla had reached the end of a shift she had wished she could plug into some of his energy reserves. Mostly, though, she had tried not to think of him at all, because he was a very distracting man.

'Mr Bruni.' The moisture clinging to his face and plastering his dark hair to his skull suggested he'd been standing there for a while.

'My name is Gianfranco.' He elevated a dark brow but Dervla was too flustered by his presence—his much too physical presence—to respond to the enquiring signal. She was painfully conscious of his continued light, casual touch on her shoulder and her response to it being anything but casual. 'Alberto calls you Dervla?'

She nodded, finding his level gaze hard to return, but discovering contrarily that she couldn't have torn her eyes from his lean, chiselled features even if her life had depended on doing so.

'Yes.'

'It is an unusual name.'

'My grandmother was Irish. I was named after her.'

He turned his head and nodded towards the grey night. 'You are going home?'

She nodded.

'And you are tired, hungry because you worked through your supper break and wondering,' he added with a flash of his wolfish smile, 'how I know these things.'

Her mouth fell open. 'How do you know?' Hidden cameras or was he psychic?

'I watch you.'

Three words, but they had roughly the same effect on Dervla as the world tilting on its axis, which, if she remembered rightly, could result in the end of all life on the planet as we knew it.

The thought of those dark eyes following her sent a rush of heat through her body. It seemed pretty pointless telling herself the empty feeling in the pit of her stomach was disgust when her skin literally tingled with illicit excitement.

'I'd be flattered if I thought there was much else for you to look at,' she said in an attempt to laugh off his comment.

It was more difficult, in fact impossible, to laugh off the expression in his dark intense eyes as they moved over her face, then drifted lower down, skimming her body.

The muscles low in Dervla's abdomen tightened and continued to flutter uncontrollably as she struggled to fight back the insidious lethargy that was stealing the strength from her limbs and making mush of her brain.

'It is never a hardship to watch a beautiful woman.'

'Me!'

Her startled exclamation drew a rumble of laughter from his chest.

'It is infinitely preferable to watch you than your friend the muscular charge nurse. You two are an item, perhaps?'

'John!' She was genuinely startled by the suggestion. 'No, of course not.'

'He watches you too.'

'Don't be ridiculous,' she retorted crossly.

'Poor John,' he said softly. 'And now I have made you think about it you realise that I am right. It is useless to deny it. You have the most transparent face I have ever seen.'

He made it sound like a flaw and Dervla was inclined to agree with him. There were thoughts going through her head at that moment she would have been happier to be ignorant of herself! The idea that she might be broadcasting them horrified her.

'You're mistaking real life for a daytime soap. I think, Mr Bruni, that you've had too much time on your hands. Your imagination has obviously got out of control.'

A slow, sensual smile tugged the corners of his mobile mouth… When it came to imagination running wild, hers got totally out of control every time she made the mistake of looking at his sinfully sexy mouth.

There was a glint in his eyes she didn't dare analyse as he readily conceded her point. 'It could be that you're right there and imagination is no substitute for reality. Not when it becomes painfully frustrating…' he murmured, staring at her soft pink lips in a way that made the knot of need low in her belly tighten.

'Actually, Mr Bruni, I find that reality rarely lives up to imagination.' His distracting mouth for instance. There was no way he was as good a kisser as those sculpted sensual lips suggested.

'That gives me no great opinion of the men in your life.'

It took a few seconds for his meaning to sink in, and when it did the colour flew to her cheeks. 'I wasn't talking about sex!'

'Of course not,' he soothed, looking amused by her outrage. 'Food is a much more comfortable subject. I thought you might like to go for something to eat—real food, not imaginary?'

She blinked up at him totally nonplussed. 'You're asking me to dinner?'

'We are both hungry and I am alone here…'

He said it with the manner of a man without a friend in the world, which was so totally implausible she almost laughed. 'And you couldn't pick up a phone or simply snap your fingers and have gorgeous, agreeable, intelligent company?'

His grin flashed. 'I thought the lonely card was worth playing,' he admitted with no trace of remorse. 'You are agreeable, intelligent company.'

'Flattery will get you nowhere.'

'So?' He arched a brow. 'You will come?'

'That's out of the question.'

'Why?'

'I'm in my uniform and you're…' She stopped, her glance sweeping upwards from his toes to the top of his glossy sable head. Oh, God, but he really was the best-looking man she had ever seen.

One corner of his mouth twitched. 'I'm what, Dervla?'

The way he said her name in that seductive velvet voice sent a rush of colour to her cheeks. She lowered her eyes. With a voice like his he could make a shopping list sound sexy.

'People like you don't go to dinner with people like me.'

People like him went to dinner with glossy long-stemmed beauties, women with blonde dead-straight hair and interesting lifestyles that did not require them under any circumstances to wear something that resembled an ill-fitting and not very flattering uniform.

'There is a law to this effect?'

Dervla pursed her lips primly, stared at her feet and thought there ought to be. She was deeply ashamed of and painfully conscious of her physical response to his overt brand of rampant raw masculinity.

'You make it sound as though we are different species, Dervla.'

'We might as well be, Mr Bruni.'

'Gianfranco.'

'It's really very kind of you, Mr Bruni, but you don't have to take me to dinner just because you bumped into me. Most relatives express their gratitude with a tin of toffees.'

'I am all out of toffees.' He held out his hands palm up to illustrate the point.

Dervla's glance moved to the long fingers extended towards her.

'And I did not bump into you; I was waiting for you.'

Her eyes flew to his face. 'Why would you do that?' she demanded, unease unfurling low in her belly. Along with it was an equally uncomfortable flutter of excitement.

'Why do men usually wait for you, Dervla?'

'They don't and will you stop calling me that?'

'Is it not your name?'

'Not the way you say it. The way you say it makes it sound like someone else.'

'Good, then act out of character and get into the car.'

She turned her head in the direction he indicated. 'What car?' How had she missed that?

The limousine with the tinted windows pulled up to the kerb beside them was massive.

She felt his hand fall on her shoulder and didn't see the harm in letting it stay there just for a minute.

'You need cheering up.'

Their eyes meshed and Dervla felt the resistance weaken as she gazed into his deep velvet brown eyes.

'I'm not in need of cheering up,' she protested, tugging her arm free. 'Seriously.'

'I am in need,' he retorted. 'Seriously.'

Something in his voice made Dervla pause in the act of pulling away. Her eyes lifted slowly, a crease of concern appearing on her brow as she registered for the first time the dark shadows under his eyes and the lines of strain etched into the skin around his mouth.

Her belligerence melted away. For some people prayer, adrenaline and caffeine took them through the early critical stages of a loved one's illness, but later, when the critical danger passed, the emotional backlash hit them. The effect could often be debilitating.

It was difficult to imagine a man less likely to rouse her maternal instincts. It was also difficult to think of one more likely to push himself too far.

'You must be very tired.' This man really doesn't need looking after, her inner voice of reason and logic pointed out.

'I could do with a change of scene. I thought you'd be pleased I was taking your advice. Isn't that what you've been telling me for days via your excellent charge nurse?' he asked innocently. 'A more sensitive man might assume you were reluctant to talk to me…?'

'I thought you might find advice easier to take if it came from a man.'

'You think I have a problem with strong women? Actually I like a woman who knows what she wants and is not afraid to tell a man.'

It could be she was hearing sexual innuendo that wasn't there. All the same she struggled to keep the blush at bay.

'Taking instruction from a woman in the right circumstances can, in my experience, be most agreeable.'

Oh, no, it was most definitely there!

She ignored the dangerous kick of excitement in her stomach and gave him a level look. It only stayed level until she saw the glitter burning deep in the dark depths. 'Don't look at me like that!'

Inside the hospital she was in control; outside there was no name badge to hide behind. Their roles were reversed and it scared her.

'Why?'

'Because I don't like it.' Not totally a lie—liking had very little to do with the shivers walking up and down her spine.

'Have dinner with me.'

'I wouldn't be good company.'

'I'll take the risk. Relax.' The advice almost made her laugh…relaxing around this man was a clinical impossibility. 'You're hungry, I'm hungry…where is the problem?'

He turned aside to speak in rapid Italian to the driver before opening the rear door of the plush vehicle for Dervla.

After a pause she slid inside. It was only a meal and sometimes you had to live a little dangerously—and all that was waiting for her at home was a microwave dinner for one.

'Gracious, this is bigger than my kitchen!' she exclaimed, too startled by the extravagant luxury to maintain any level of nonchalance. 'You're not worried about your green credentials, then.' This monster had to have a gigantic carbon footprint.

'I would be a poor businessman if I wasn't—'

'And not a "ruthless financial genius",' she quoted with a twinkle.

He shook his head and gave a rueful grin. 'That Sunday supplement quote will, I suspect, go with me to my grave.'

'Is this the way a genius travels?'

'I am no genius and I generally find it more convenient to use a helicopter.'

The retort drew a laugh from her. 'What about ruthless?' she asked curiously.

His charismatic smile flashed. 'That rather depends on who you're talking to.'

'I'm talking to you.'

'What do you think?'

'I think you can't give a straight answer. Perhaps you should go into politics.'

'So you want to know the man behind the trashy headline?'

She shook her head. 'I don't have that sort of time.' This man was so complicated that she suspected it would take a very long time to even begin to work out the kinks in his personality. 'This is just one dinner date.'

His dark lashes lifted from the razor-sharp angle of his sculpted cheekbones. Dervla's stomach flipped as their eyes connected.

'It doesn't have to be one dinner date.'

The earthy warmth in his steady scrutiny made her stomach flip. She tried to laugh to reduce the tension that had sprung up in the confined space, but her vocal cords were paralysed.

'You are probably right not to commit yourself. Wait and see how this evening goes.'

CHAPTER EIGHT

DERVLA wanted to tell Gianfranco that the evening was going nowhere but the excitement circulating in her bloodstream resisted her efforts. Her heart was thudding so loud that she was sure he must be able to hear it.

A few moments later their sumptuous ride drew to a halt—an abrupt halt, and equally abruptly Dervla shot forward. She gave a knee-jerk scream and closed her eyes as impact with the glass panel separating them from the driver seemed inevitable.

At the last moment she found herself pulled backwards, anchored to the seat by an arm like a steel band around her waist.

The glass partition slid down and the driver's anxious face appeared. 'Sorry about that. A dog ran out,' he said, speaking excellent English but with a more pronounced Italian accent than his employer.

'You avoided it?'

The driver nodded. 'Lucky you were wearing seat belts back there.'

'Very lucky,' Gianfranco agreed, his sardonic gaze levelled on Dervla's guilty face.

The glass partition closed and while the driver got out to open the passenger doors Gianfranco's arm slid from her waist.

He was still so close she could feel the heat of his body and smell the shampoo he used on his silky ebony hair. She struggled against a sudden crazy impulse to sink her fingers into that lush pelt.

'I always wear my seat belt,' she said defensively.

'Clearly not always…'

Her breath came a little easier as he moved away, but every nerve ending in her body remained painfully inflamed. 'Well, always before today.'

She turned her head and connected with his dark eyes.

Her rueful smile guttered.

His eyes were blazing, a nerve beside his clenched mouth throbbing and the bruises on his forehead stood out livid against his deathly pallor. Gianfranco looked incandescent with rage.

'Are you a total fool?'

Dervla's first instinct was to defend herself against his blighting scorn, but it was pretty hard to defend the indefensible.

'How many people have you seen brought into Casualty after going head first through windscreens?'

From his expression Dervla suspected he had witnessed such an event himself, maybe even been personally involved, which would explain his somewhat dramatic reaction to the incident.

'All right, I should know better,' she admitted, shamefaced.

'That face could have been…' His chest lifted as he dragged in deep before he reached across and placed one big hand around the curve of her cheek. A distracted expression drifted into his deepset eyes as he rubbed his thumb in a circular motion across the apple of her cheek.

Dervla, mesmerized, stared up at him, her eyes half closed as the friction of his thumb against her skin increased the growing liquid ache low in her pelvis.

'Next time I might not be there to save you. Promise me,' he demanded huskily, 'that you will never do that again.'

Dervla had no trouble supplying the promise he demanded, but she did have trouble making it audible as her enraptured eyes stayed locked on his lean face, her throat clogged with emotion she couldn't put a name to.

The opening of the limo door provided the necessary distraction to allow her to escape the sensual thrall that held her immobilised and break free of that intense stare.

Dervla was so flustered that she didn't immediately register as she stepped out into the damp night that there were no eateries, casual or otherwise, in the residential square.

'This isn't a restaurant,' she said, levelling an accusing glare at him as they approached the porticoed entrance of a large Georgian building.

'This is my house.'

'Which part?'

'All of it.'

She rolled her eyes. 'Of course it is.'

The door was opened before they reached it. A dark-haired woman in her thirties wearing a navy skirt smiled pleasantly at Dervla, who, impelled forward by firm hand in the small of her back, stepped forward into the elegant hallway lit by chandeliers and dominated by a sweeping staircase a full orchestra could have been neatly tucked away beneath.

Dazzled by all the gleaming splendour, she didn't catch the name as Gianfranco introduced his housekeeper. After a brief exchange in Italian the soft-voiced older woman bid them a polite goodnight and vanished through one of the many doors that opened onto the reception area.

'Come.'

Left with little choice Dervla did as he bid, though his autocratic manner really grated on her. He led her through a series of doors and down a long corridor. When they reached the end he opened the door and signalled for her to precede him.

Dervla stepped inside. It was a kitchen, though not like any kitchen she knew. The only place she had seen rooms like this was in the pages of glossy magazines. She ran a hand across the surface of a tall larder unit, the burred-oak finish smooth under her fingers.

'This is the kitchen.'

'Well spotted,' he approved, slinging a quick ironic grin in her direction as he slid off his jacket. 'You like risotto?'

Dervla stared as he pulled open the doors of a massive fridge and began to extract ingredients. 'You cook?'

'That surprises you?'

'It frankly surprises me that you know where the kitchen is.'

He laughed, the crinkly lines around his eyes deepening.

Oh, help, he is so attractive!

He looked, she decided, more relaxed than she had ever seen him, but given the environment she had seen him in up to this point perhaps that was not so very surprising.

'Don't you have a chef?'

'Several. I also have a driver, but that doesn't mean I can't drive a car. Though my lifestyle does not allow me the opportunity to practise my culinary skills as often as I would like. Why does that make you laugh? Do you not believe I can cook?'

'Oh, it's not that.' She was quite prepared to believe he could do anything. 'You have several chefs and think that's normal… It's just you're so super-rich…' Hands outstretched, she looked around the gleaming, stylish room. 'It's as if you live on another planet.'

He gave a fluid shrug. 'We live on the same planet, Dervla. The important things in life still have no price tag.'

'Unlike that little lot,' she observed, nodding towards the gleaming state-of-the-art equipment.

'The chef likes his gadgets, but I hope you do not think worse of me that I prefer a slightly more…hands-on approach. But a good knife, that is a different matter.' He took a chef's knife from a wooden block and balanced it lightly in his hand.

The less she thought about his hands, the better, Dervla

decided, sucking a deep sustaining breath before she admitted, 'I'll take your word for it. I'm more of a microwave-meal girl myself.'

'I honestly don't spend much time in the kitchen myself,' he admitted. 'But when I do I find it relaxing. The secret of a good risotto is the stock,' he said, rolling up his sleeves, and for the second time that day her attention was drawn to the sinewy strength in his forearms.

Actually she was pretty much riveted by him full stop. 'Can I do anything?' Like worship at your feet? suggested the sarcastic voice in her head.

'You can take off your coat, pour us some wine…the wine cooler is just to your left.' He tilted his dark head towards a glass-fronted cabinet. 'And make yourself comfortable.'

He tugged out a chair beside the scrubbed table he had placed his ingredients on. Slipping her damp coat off, she folded it across a chair back and, dropping down to her knees, opened the cooler. 'What wine?' she asked, feeling totally out of her depth as she stared at the bewildering array of wines on display.

'Just close your eyes and take pot luck,' he suggested, before turning his attention to an onion that he proceeded to dice with professional speed. 'Corkscrew,' he added, reaching into a drawer to his right and tossing the item in question towards her. 'Good catch.'

Dervla opened the bottle after a short tussle and filled the two glasses. Sitting in a chair, she set her elbows on the table and, nursing her glass of wine, watched as he continued to chop, slice and stir with economic dexterity.

It was not long before the room was filled with a nose-twitching smell.

'That looks good.'

His eyes lifted from his creation. 'You hungry?'

She nodded. Actually the empty feeling in her churning stomach had no connection with anything as simple as hunger.

'Good.' He lifted a spoon to his lips, gave a critical nod of approval. 'About done. If you stir it I'll set the table. Don't worry, it won't bite,' he added, looking amused as she looked at the spoon suspiciously.

'That's it, just keep it moving.' His fingers brushed hers as he released the spoon to her and the light contact sent a surge of tingling lust through her body that excited and terrified her.

What am I doing here? I don't belong in this world. She turned her head to look at him through the silky sweep of her lashes and thought, His world. This is his world and I don't belong in it.

'Have a seat.' He pulled out a chair and motioned her to sit as he lit the candle he had produced from somewhere.

Soft music and it would be the classic seduction scene.

Even the faintest possibility should have had her running for the door, but she wasn't running. Her heart was beating faster, she felt breathless, almost light-headed.

Anyone would think I wanted to be seduced.

She rejected the idea with a tiny shake of her head. She had never been tempted by casual relationships; the idea of intimacy without love left her cold.

So why was her skin crackling with heat?

'You really didn't have to go to so much trouble on my account,' she said, staring into the flickering flame worriedly.

'It was my pleasure.'

She turned her head and saw he was watching her, his mouth curved into a sardonic smile. She had the horrible feeling he knew exactly what she was thinking.

'But as I have gone to so much trouble, it would be churlish of you not to eat the results of my hard labour,' he chided softly.

Not quite meeting his eyes, Dervla shivered inside, flashed him a half-smile and took her seat.

She would eat and leave. She was in danger, she told herself, of overcomplicating this, making way too much of a casual glance or an ambiguous comment. She had to stop seeing things that weren't there.

Gianfranco took the seat opposite. He bent forward to top up her glass, but she shook her head and murmured quickly. 'Not for me.'

She noticed he didn't replenish his own glass either. He made no effort to pick up his fork, but waited, elbows pressed on the table, his chin resting on his hands, for her to try the food.

'Well?'

'It's delicious,' she admitted truthfully. 'Are you going back to the hospital tonight?'

He shook his head. 'No, Alberto has asserted his independence and thrown me out.'

'He has more guts than the rest of us.'

While they ate the subjects of conversation remained similar safe, desultory topics and Dervla began to—relax was too strong a word, but her defences lowered slightly and the tension slipped out of her rigid spine. But all the time they spoke and said little she was still very conscious that this was Gianfranco Bruni who was a dangerous man accustomed to getting what he wanted.

And if he wants me?

Dervla took a jittery gasp and got to her feet so quickly that she almost knocked her chair over.

'That was lovely, but it is late.' Late to pretend she wasn't attracted to him and hadn't been from the moment she had laid eyes on him. 'I really should be going.' I really should never have come.

Gianfranco set aside his napkin and rose with the fluid grace that typified all his actions.

'It's early,' he protested, walking around to her side of the table.

Dervla stood there, her heart hammering, twisting the white linen napkin in her hands, her feet nailed to the ground as he came to stand beside her, close enough for her to feel the heat radiating from his body.

She kept her eyes trained on her half-full glass on the table. 'I really should…'

Do You Have the LUCKY KEY?

PLAY THE Lucky Key Game

and you can get

FREE BOOKS and FREE GIFTS!

Scratch the gold areas with a coin. Then check below to see the books and gifts you can get!

YES!

I have scratched off the gold areas. Please send me the 2 FREE BOOKS and 2 FREE GIFTS, worth about $10, for which I qualify. I understand I am under no obligation to purchase any books, as explained on the back of this card.

306 HDL ERR6   106 HDL ERVV

FIRST NAME   LAST NAME

ADDRESS

APT.#   CITY

STATE/PROV.   ZIP/POSTAL CODE

www.eHarlequin.com

2 free books plus 2 free gifts   1 free book

2 free books   Try Again!

He touched his thumb to the full outline of her lower lip and she started violently, her questioning sea-green eyes lifting.

'Your mouth—it looks so soft and lush.'

Their eyes connected and the heat and hunger Dervla saw reflected in the dark surface of his sent a sensual shock wave along her tingling nerve endings.

'This evening isn't going where you seem to think it is,' she blurted, pressing a hand to her breastbone. Behind it her heart was trying to batter its way to freedom.

He arched a sardonic brow. 'Where would that be?'

She shook her head, finding it hard to catch her breath. 'I'm not really a one-night stand sort of person.'

'One night would not be nearly enough.'

The throaty observation drew a faint whimper from her throat that she tried to cover with a brittle laugh. 'I really don't think being seen in the right places with me would do your reputation any good.'

'I'm not interested in my reputation and the only place I am interested in seeing you is in my bed.'

His head tilted to one side, he studied her burning face. 'I've shocked you? You are not comfortable with discussing sex.'

'I find this entire conversation very uncomfortable.'

'You would prefer we discuss the weather? We could do but we would both be thinking about sex.'

She lifted her chin and fixed him with a defiant stare. 'Speak for yourself.'

'You disappoint me. You did not strike me as a hypocrite.'

The charge drew an angry grunt from Dervla, who stood rigidly upright beside him, her fingers busy pleating the napkin. 'I'm not a hypocrite, but neither am I oversexed.'

The opposite was in fact true…at least it had been until now. Right now her libido had gone global. She had her hands clasped because she couldn't trust herself not to rip off his clothes.

He bent his head, his breath stirring the soft downy hair on her cheek. 'You want me,' he said, his voice low and thick. 'And you know I want you and you like that. It excites you. I excite you.'

She shook her head, knowing that if she spoke she might give the impression she wanted him to carry on saying these things, that she wanted him to do a lot of things.

And didn't she?

She shook her head again, scared rigid by the intensity of the feelings crowding in.

'I've wanted to kiss you for the past week. I'm going to do it now if that's all right with you…?'

His seductive voice made things shudder deep inside her. He wasn't asking permission, he was just igniting the sparks and expertly feeding the escalating sexual tension another few notches with his honied voice. He didn't actually expect her to say no because women had been saying yes to him all his life.

And it looks like I'm no different.

And she wasn't different—for him this was sex with no obligations. Recognising it didn't make her feel any the less desperate for him. She made a last-ditch attempt to walk away.

'It really is very late.' Even she could hear the lack of conviction in her whispered protest.

'What's the hurry? You're not on duty in the morning.'

'How do you know?'

'I checked.'

'Why would you do that?'

One corner of his fascinating mouth lifted in a lazy smile as he touched his forefinger to her cheek. 'Information is power, Dervla.' His hand fell away but the dark itch under her skin didn't.

She wanted him to touch her.

She lifted her chin and tried to look amused. 'You've got no power over me.' Shame her hormones were not equally autonomous.

'Pity, you've got me in the palm of your lovely little hand.'

He took her wrist and peeled back her clenched fingers like the petals of a flower. His heavy-lidded eyes lifted to her face as he whispered throatily, 'A very pretty hand.'

His touch was inflicting terrible, probably irreparable damage to her nervous system. Wide eyes welded with a mixture of fear and longing to his strong face, she released a long shuddering sigh and admitted, 'I don't really want to go.'

Something flared deep in his eyes, primitive male satisfaction shot through with something less easily identifiable.

'Then stay, *cara*.'

'But I'm not even sure I like you.'

He laughed, throwing back his head to reveal the strong column of his brown throat. 'If it makes you feel any better, for the first twenty-four hours I was pretty sure that I disliked you.'

'You didn't hide it very well.' She tried to smile and couldn't—her throat ached with emotion.

'I wanted sex with you even when I disliked you.' His lips twisted into a smile. 'You look shocked again.'

Her lashes lowered. She felt excited, which was far more disturbing. 'I am shocked that I'm doing this.'

Her breath came in short painful gasps as he leaned forward and bent his dark head to hers. This close she could see the gold tips on his long dark lashes and the fine texture of his golden skin. As he got closer still things went out of focus like a kaleidoscope and the wild beating of her heart became louder and faster.

Anticipation tightened like a fist low in her belly as her lips parted under the gentle but insistent pressure of his mouth.

As his tongue slid into her mouth Dervla moaned low in her throat and grabbed his shoulders, plastering herself up against his lean, hard, vital body as she kissed him back with an eagerness that was close to desperation.

'*Dio Mio!*' He drew a ragged breath and angled his head to look into her face as they finally broke apart. 'You are everything I imagined and much, much more.'

The glow of dark desire she could see shimmering in his eyes took her breath away and made her head spin even before his lips began to move once more with sensual teasing persuasion against her soft mouth. His hand moved to the curve of her breast and Dervla's knees turned to water.

'Not enough!' she moaned after a few minutes of this torture.

Gianfranco dragged his mouth away from hers fractionally and, breathing hard, he studied her flushed, aroused features. 'Not enough of what?' he asked thickly.

Dervla sighed and ran the tip of her tongue across the sensual curve of his upper lip. 'You,' she confided.

'You want more of me?'

Eyes dilated, she tilted her head back to bring his dark features into focus. 'No, I want all of you.'

Gianfranco sucked in a deep breath through flared nostrils and, winding his fingers into her bright hair, pulled her head farther back, exposing the long graceful curve of her pale throat.

Dervla's lids drifted closed as he pressed his lips to the hollow at the base of her throat and then made his way by means of a series of erotic kisses up to her mouth.

She gave a startled little cry as he suddenly swung her up into his arms. 'What are you doing?'

He strode towards the door and kicked it open. 'I don't want the first time to be on the kitchen table.'

'I don't mind where it is so long as it happens.' Did I just say that?

CHAPTER NINE

BREATHING hard, but not, it would seem, from the exertion of running up two flights of stairs carrying her—Gianfranco had taken them two at a time and not shown any signs of fatigue— he kicked open the door to this huge bedroom dominated by a large four-poster.

Probably the rest of the furnishings were just as impressive but Dervla was not actually interested in the décor. Her entire attention was focused on the man who laid her down carefully in the middle of the vast bed, before switching on a lamp.

He was still breathing hard as, kneeling on the bed, he tugged his shirt from his trousers and fought his way out of it.

Dervla's gasp was audible. Desire clutched low in her belly as she stared at him in silent awe.

He was hard and sleek, his golden streamlined body carrying not an ounce of flesh to blur the perfection of the muscle definition in his chest and ridged, hair-roughened stomach.

She wanted to touch him, feel his bare skin against her own; she wanted to taste him, and feel his hands on her body. She wasn't aware that she had expressed her growing desperation to fulfil these ambitions until he slipped the buckle on his belt and promised in a throaty drawl, 'You will, *cara*, you will...' His eyes didn't leave her face for a second as he slid his trousers down over his narrow hips and kicked them away. He stood there for a moment wearing just a pair of boxers that did little to disguise the strength of his arousal.

Propped up on one elbow, he arranged his long lean length alongside her. He trailed a line of kisses down the curve of her jaw as he reached for the hem of her top.

Dervla gave a sensuous little wriggle to assist him as he lifted it over her head and flung it across the room.

Feeling the air on her overheated skin and enjoying the sensation, she laid her hands flat on his belly and felt the convulsive contraction of muscles underneath his silky, hair-roughened skin.

'You have bruises,' she whispered, her eyes darkening as she traced the uneven outline of one of the livid areas of discolouration along the crest of his right hipbone. 'It must have been agony!' she accused, thinking of how he had maintained his silent vigil.

'No,' he said, taking her hand in his and moving it lower. 'This was agony,' he contradicted thickly. 'This is agony,' he rasped throatily as he pulsed hard and hot against the constraints of her hand.

He didn't just fill her hand but her mind and soul, stretching her emotional capacity to the limit and onto a new, mind-expanding level.

'You're the only medicine I needed, or wanted. I knew that I would find the comfort I needed in your body.'

There was dark colour scoring his jutting cheekbones as he held himself above her, staring with hot, hungry eyes at the rapid rise and fall of her straining breasts inside their lacy covering.

'Virginal white,' he murmured, his smile inviting her to share the joke as he reached for the front-fastening clasp.

Some joke!

The unintentional reminder made Dervla tense, but then his hands were cupping her bare breasts, weighing them in his big hands. The incredible sensation left little room in her pleasure-soaked brain for misgivings.

Her eyes drifted closed as she listened to his accented voice, telling her she was perfect and sounding flatteringly shaken about the discovery.

Any residual qualms totally vaporised when his thumb began to tease first one straining peak and then the other into burning life before he applied his lips and tongue to the same task.

Convulsed with pleasure, her entire body responding to his lightest touch and caress, she was barely aware of his stripping away first her jeans and then her lacy-edged pants until she felt his fingers slide into the bright curls at the apex of her legs, searching for the slick, hot centre of her.

Dervla shuddered with a nameless need as he pressed soft kisses to her closed eyelids and touched the tight, throbbing, sensitised flesh at her centre. The shockingly intimate invasion drew a keening cry of startled pleasure from her tight, aching throat. His caresses took her to the brink of something outside her experience but he pulled back quite literally before she crested the peak.

'Oh, God, I'm…'

'You're perfect; we're perfect,' he told her before he slid down her body, kissing his way down the gentle curve of her stomach. 'This,' he added, kneeling between her parted thighs, 'will be perfect too.'

Dervla sighed as she stared greedily at his magnificent glistening naked body. She didn't doubt for a moment his ability to deliver perfect in many forms. It was only her doubts concerning her ability to fulfil his apparently pretty high expectations of her that brought a faint frown to her damp brow.

'I have to have you… Dervla, you are driving me out of my mind.'

She responded by looping her arms around his neck, arching her back and pressing her bare breasts provocatively to his chest.

She was conscious of his breath hot on her neck as he pushed his way past the swollen lips of her resisting flesh and into her.

Her body arched under him and a sigh of amazement was wrenched from the very depths of her being.

'*Per amor di Dio!*'

Barely even conscious of his stricken exclamation, Dervla wrapped her legs around his hips and clung onto his sweat-slick shoulders. At some level she did register the tremors that shook his big body as he held himself in check, but there were so many other incredible things happening that mostly she just registered how unbelievable it felt to have him hard and thick inside her.

'This is incredible, you're…oh, my—!' she gasped as he sank a little deeper.

She cried his name over and over like a litany as he filled an emptiness she hadn't known existed inside her, sinking deeper into her silken tightness, coaxing her towards the moment of total fulfilment, his own body shaking with the effort his restraint cost.

Then in the final moments as she hovered on the brink he ditched that restraint and with a cry plunged into her until they both reached the splintering climax simultaneously.

As he shuddered into her in the final convulsions of release she gave herself to him without reserve.

'Oh, Gianfranco!' she gasped, taking his face between her hands and pressing a fervent kiss to his lips. 'You have no idea how glad I am I stayed. You are totally perfect.' He actually looked like a man who had just been hit by a thunderbolt, but what did she know? That was probably normal. With a sleepy sigh she curled up in his arms and gave a contented sigh.

'We are here.' The chauffeur consulted his watch. 'The ferry is due in five minutes. Would you like me to meet Alberto?'

Dragging herself kicking and screaming back to the present, Dervla struggled to escape the power of the erotic recollections. There was a tinge of guilt to her smile as she shook her head and touched a shaky hand to her hot, flushed cheeks.

She cleared her throat, struggling to regain her composure as she replied, 'Thanks, Eduardo. I'll meet him myself.'

A cold shower not being an option, she could really do with some fresh air!

As she was stepping out of the car Gianfranco was consulting his watch as he pulled into the fast lane of the motorway. His private jet had got him into the country before his son and by his calculations, barring any major snarl-up on the way, he ought to be in London a full thirty minutes before his runaway wife and son reached the house.

His expression hardened as he contemplated the inevitable confrontation that lay ahead.

She had behaved badly. Gianfranco was consumed by coruscating anger every time he considered her crazy conduct. But even while he condemned her he knew that his own actions might not stand up to strong scrutiny.

In his more rational moments—pretty few and far between over the last couple of days—he knew some might consider he was a more legitimate target for the anger he directed towards Dervla.

He had married her when he knew she wanted more than he was able or willing to give. Hadn't something like this been inevitable?

But she knew the ground rules…and he refused to acknowledge what he felt for her was more than lust. Strong lust certainly, but nothing more. He repudiated the sly suggestion from the argumentative voice in his head that he'd been selfish to marry her.

Selfish? He'd given her everything she'd asked for—not that she had ever asked for anything except his support and advice in getting the hospice off the ground.

So if she asked for her freedom you'd let her go? Let her find a man she deserves, because she deserves better than you!

What, and let her loose to be the target of the first unscrupulous bastard with slick patter and a hard-luck story? His jaw tautened as, with an aggressive snort of disgust, he treated the ridiculous idea with the contempt it deserved.

At least with him she was safe.

The problem was she was so damned giving.

And she had given it all to him, held nothing back.

He would never forget that moment when he had realised he had seduced a virgin.

Sure, you were so traumatised you only paused to catch your breath before trying to do it again!

Ignoring the sardonic interjection of the critical voice in his head, Gianfranco recalled the primitive surge of male satisfaction tinged by a tenderness that had followed his initial blank shock.

When he had held her in his arms and told her that the possibility that she would be a virgin had never even crossed his mind she had confirmed her naivety by saying with a rueful grimace, 'You noticed, then. I was wondering if you would.'

'How is this possible? You are twenty-six. I thought I was a late starter,' he muttered under his breath.

With feline grace that fascinated him, she rolled over and snuggled with a very un-virginlike lack of self-consciousness up to him. She trailed a finger down his sweat-slick hair-roughened chest, insinuating the feminine curve of her hip into the hard angle of his as she threw one slim thigh across his legs.

'So how old were you?' she asked, adding with a sigh of voluptuous pleasure and a sexy shimmy of her soft body against his, 'God, this is good and you are totally and absolutely beautiful.' Her exuberance was contagious.

'Are you going to fall asleep?'

'No, I am not going to fall asleep,' he promised, laughing.

He had never associated laughter with sex before, but then it was not his habit to indulge in teasing banter or snuggling in the post-coital aftermath.

The romantic boy in him was long dead. For him sex was about satisfying a mutual primal need. Modern society felt the need to dress it up and talk of spiritual, emotional connections, but he did not buy into the self-deception.

And if on occasion, no matter how great the sex had been, he was left with a vague feeling of dissatisfaction, not being a man inclined towards introspection, he didn't analyse it or feel he was missing out on anything.

'So how old were you?' she persisted.

'You seem fascinated by my sexual history.'

Tongue caught between her teeth, she trailed a finger down his chest, her green eyes teasing him from under the flirtatious sweep of her lashes. It amused him to see her discovering the power of her female sexuality and taking such obvious delight from it—so was he!

Her questing hand slid lower and she gave a deliciously throaty chuckle as he shuddered, his body stirring lustfully.

'I'm fascinated by lots of things about you,' she admitted. 'But I did have you down as a *very* early starter.'

Very conscious of the small hand that now rested palm down on the flat of his belly, he retorted, 'I was not twenty-six.' He avoided whenever possible thinking of his idealistic nineteen-year-old self.

'How is it possible that a woman who looks like you has never had a lover?'

'Thank you. That's a very nice thing to say. You've got lovely manners.'

'Manners? *Dio*, you say the oddest things. It's not *nice*; it is a fact—you are beautiful.' He caught her softly rounded chin in his hand and tilted her heart-shaped face up to him and looked deep into her emerald eyes.

Dervla didn't look away, but looked steadily back at him, though there was a touch of shyness in her direct gaze. When he touched his thumb to her lips, still swollen from his kisses, and traced the cushiony softness, her lashes had swept downwards, brushing against her smooth flushed cheeks.

He kissed the delicate blue-veined eyelids and murmured, '*Very* beautiful *and* desirable. I thought so from the moment I saw you.'

Her eyelashes lifted and there was a sparkle of teasing wickedness in her eyes. 'Do you want to know what I thought when I first saw you?' Before he could respond she shook her head and with a rueful grimace said, 'On second thoughts, don't ask. It wasn't very professional.'

He watched her expression grow sober, a furrow appearing between her feathery brows as she touched the sutures that had closed the healing wound that lay close to the hairline at his right temple and ended at his jaw.

He caught her hand and raised it to his lips.

'Come to think of it, *this* isn't very professional,' she said huskily as she curled her fingers around his jaw. He watched the clear green of her marvellous eyes cloud as, with a distracted expression, she began to stroke her thumb across the light dusting of stubble on his cheek.

'But what you lacked in expertise you made up for in enthusiasm.'

It took her a second before she digested his comment; in the next second her eyes widened as she loosed an indignant, 'You know what I mean!' before she rolled away from him and in one seamless motion pulled herself into a sitting position. Then, balancing on her heels, she lobbed a pillow at his chest.

Gianfranco had been too absorbed by the gentle and incredibly erotic quiver of her small pink-tipped breasts to block the missile.

Pleased that he had succeeded in driving the self-recriminatory frown from her face, he grinned, removed the second weapon from her hands and pushed her back against the mattress. Supported above her by one hand, he curved the other over her delectable bottom. As he dragged her to him he heard her sharp intake of breath and felt the vibration as the husky little whimper got trapped in her throat.

Looking into her eyes, he saw them dilate dramatically until just a thin ring of green remained. She aroused a hunger in him that threatened the control he prided himself on.

'What you need, *cara*, is practice and lots of it.'

'Which you will provide?' Before he could assure her of his total willingness to do so she suddenly groaned. 'No, this is all wrong!'

'Wrong?' It felt pretty right to him. Frustration clawed at his belly.

'Patients are vulnerable,' she explained solemnly. 'Sometimes they get close to the people caring for them, imagine they have feelings.' Her eyes slid from his. 'It's a well-documented fact. To take advantage of someone vulnerable is despicable… and I can't even claim I didn't know what I was doing. I knew exactly what I was doing.'

It took him a few seconds to interpret her convoluted and earnest explanation.

'You think you are taking advantage of me?' He had to bite back the laughter because she clearly took this very seriously. 'If anyone could be accused of taking advantage it should be me. You were the virgin.' She brushed aside the reminder with a wave of her hand. 'And today you were upset because you lost your patient.'

'I'm a nurse and I work on a unit where people are very ill, patients die.'

'And you stay objective—you expect me to believe that?' he asked incredulously. 'I've watched you.' He actually couldn't take his eyes off her. 'You ooze empathy.'

She gave him a quizzical look. 'Is that a bad thing?'

'Not for the lonely old man you visited on your day off.'

'Mr Chambers had no family here. His daughter had emigrated, she was coming and—'

'You do not need to explain your actions to me, Dervla. I am not your patient.'

'No, but your son is.'

'Not for much longer.' If Alberto threw off the infection that had slightly delayed his progress, the medics said he ought to be fit enough to be transferred to a hospital within half an hour's drive from their Florence home to convalesce.

She nodded. 'You'll be home soon.'

He watched as without warning tears started to leak from Dervla's glorious eyes. 'My God,' she groaned, flashing him a mortified look as she brushed them away. 'I'm so sorry.'

'Why are you crying, Dervla?' he asked, sitting upright.

Normally tears were his cue for recalling he needed to be somewhere else. Gianfranco had a cynical take on female tears, being of the opinion they were more to do with manipulation than sentiment.

Only it was fast dawning on him that unlike other lovers in his past, this redhead didn't know the first thing about manipulation or, for that matter, self-preservation.

His hands clenched into fists as he thought of her walking like an innocent lamb into the clutches of some bastard who would take advantage of that trusting nature.

Some might say she already has. Gianfranco dismissed the thought. Men took advantage of a woman when they pretended to feel something they didn't. He did not play those games.

'I'm not. I don't cry. Oh, God!' she snapped, rounding on him angrily. 'Can't a girl sniff without a full-scale interrogation?'

'You're upset and I want to know why.' He had felt a slight twinge of unease, recognising that he genuinely did want to know.

In previous relationships the most personal details he had felt it necessary to learn about the women in his life were their preferences in designer labels. He was not an ungenerous lover, but he was not one who was interested in emotionally high-maintenance women.

'Are you regretting this?'

'Regretting?' she echoed, looking startled by the suggestion and then wryly amused as she told him, 'Nothing could be farther from the truth.'

He was relieved but perplexed by the odd inflection in her voice. 'Then why…?'

She shook her head mutely and rolled away, presenting him with her slim bare back. A hand on her shoulder, he pulled her back. 'Look at me!' he commanded.

After a moment she did. Their eyes meshed and the silence stretched until a small choking sound escaped her throat. In one single fluid motion she was on her feet at the side of the bed, red hair falling in a silken skein around her shoulders. She seemed oblivious to her nakedness as she stood there literally quivering, her pale skin glowing with an opalescent sheen.

Gianfranco had known at that moment that the image of her standing there would always remain in his memory.

'I was trying very hard to be grown up about this, but if you want to know, fine!' She flung up her arms, causing her small pink-tipped breasts to bounce in a way that sent a fresh distracting stab of lust slamming through Gianfranco's aroused body.

'I was crying because I'll miss you when you go back home.' She screwed her eyes tight shut and shook her head before fixing him with a challenging glare. 'And before you say it, *yes*, I do know how stupid that sounds and how ludicrous I'm being. I barely even know you. We have *nothing* in common and—'

'You'll *miss* me?' He watched as dull colour ran up under her fair skin as she reached for a quilt that had fallen to the ground and wrapped it around herself.

'I really don't know what I'm saying. This has been a pretty emotional day.'

Was she referring to losing the patient she had cared for or losing her virginity? He patted the bed. It was an invitation she accepted after a moment, though to his regret the quilt stayed in place as she sat primly on the edge of the bed.

'Come with me,' he heard himself say.

Her expression mirrored the incomprehension he was feeling. *'Come…?'*

'Come with us when we go back to Italy.'

'That's very nice of you, but I don't have any annual leave left this year.'

'For the record, Dervla, I am not a nice man, and I'm not talking about taking a vacation. You'd like Italy.'

'Live there, you mean?'

'Why not?'

'A hundred *why nots*,' she retorted, trying to laugh but sounding strained as she reminded him, 'My work is here, Gianfranco.'

'There are hospitals in Italy.'

'I don't speak Italian, it takes time to learn a language and I need to earn a living… God, will you listen to me?' she exclaimed, clapping a hand to her head and rolling her eyes. 'I sound as though I'm actually considering it.'

'You don't need to worry about earning a living straight away—I'm not exactly a poor man.'

Beside him she stiffened. 'You're suggesting I should pack in my job, leave my friends and come with you to Italy as your *mistress*?'

'Not mistress precisely,' he admitted.

But now that he thought about it he could see the very definite advantages to this plan. It wasn't until she turned her head and he saw her expression that it dawned on him that Dervla was not warmed to the idea.

He continued to study her and thought about the women, he could think of several, who might manage to simulate a *little* enthusiasm at the prospect of the lap of luxury as his mistress.

'Well, what else would you call a woman when a man pays

her bills in return, of course, for certain *favours*?' she enquired with withering contempt. Her bosom heaved as she choked. 'I've never been so insulted in my life!'

Her anger seemed totally inexplicable to Gianfranco. '*You* are insulted?'

He wondered whether to inform her that the post that apparently filled her with such disgust was one that any number of women had angled for over the years.

'Damn right,' she ground through clenched teeth. 'Do I seem to you like the sort of woman who would make herself reliant on a man? A woman who would give up her independence? Waiting until I'm twenty-six to discover sex might in retrospect make me a fool, but not that much of a fool.'

'So is that it? Now that you have discovered sex, you are anxious to experiment.' An image of the faceless men who would continue the education he had begun flashed into his head. The throbbing in his temples became a pulsating thud.

After staring at him in stunned silence for a moment, she threw back her head and laughed. Her eyes were sparkling with anger as she said in a flat little voice, 'And I have you to thank for my sexual liberation.'

'Do not confuse promiscuity with liberation,' he counselled severely, still seeing that line of predatory faceless males.

'*You're* accusing *me* of being promiscuous? That's rich! That really is rich! The way I hear, you change women the same way a normal man changes his shirt. If you were a woman and not filthy rich people would call you some very nasty names. And they might be right!'

'*Dio mio!*' he breathed wrathfully. The women he took to his bed were experts at pleasing a man; they did not go out of their way to insult him.

It turned out she hadn't finished with him yet.

'You know, you're the sort of man who can't talk about his feelings and thinks it's a sign of strength.'

'Suddenly you know an awful lot about men—and me,' he observed grimly.

She glared at him through shimmering green eyes and tossed her head contemptuously. 'I know enough about you to know I never want to see you again.' Snatching up her scattered clothes, she ran from the room.

He told himself that the turn of events, while frustrating, was for the best in the long run. Dervla Smith was too high maintenance. He threw aside the covers and vaulted to his feet, his toe caught in the lacy strap of her bra.

He returned it a week later when he proposed.

CHAPTER TEN

DERVLA'S apprehension increased as the limo pulled into the underground parking space of the London house. She swallowed past the nervous constriction in her throat as the car came to a halt and Eduardo switched off the engine.

Beside her Alberto clicked free his seat belt, nothing in his manner suggesting he shared her apprehension. Dervla couldn't believe he was really that relaxed, but if he wasn't, she thought, studying his stress-free, handsome young face, he was the world's best actor.

Her brow furrowed; his attitude totally baffled her. Gianfranco might be an indulgent parent, but when Alberto overstepped the mark he came down hard. And by anyone's definition he had overstepped the mark this time!

His father was going to go ballistic and Alberto had to know it.

She waited until Eduardo was out of hearing distance before she voiced the question that was uppermost in her mind.

'Why did you do it?'

He had fed her a steady stream of information concerning the highlights of his journey, including the complicated romantic life of the lorry driver who had given him a lift to Calais—she might suggest he didn't share that little anecdote with his father—but so far he hadn't even hinted at any reason for the escapade.

Alberto looked at her and shrugged.

She sucked in a sharp breath. The similarity between father and son had never been more pronounced as the teenager slung her a look from under well-defined sable brows. 'An impulse, I guess.'

Dervla rolled her eyes and begged with a groan, 'Please don't say that to your father, Alberto.'

'Don't worry about Dad, Dervla. I can handle him.'

Dervla's mouth fell open. 'You can handle…' She began to laugh. The person had not been born who could handle Gianfranco.

The boy was not offended by her amusement. 'It's all right, really, Dervla. I've got it all under control.'

'Have you suffered a head injury?' Concussion would go some way to explaining his ill-judged confidence. 'Sometimes, Alberto, there is a fine line between confidence and stupidity—in this instance there is a dirty great chasm!'

Alberto laughed.

'Alberto!' she protested. 'This isn't a joke. You can't just run away.'

'Why not, Dervla? You did.'

The gentle reminder made her flush to the roots of her hair. 'That,' she retorted, her eyes sliding from his, 'is not the same at all. I'm an adult…'

'And you're married and I'm not.'

Dervla was starting to wonder who was meant to be defending reckless behaviour here. 'Your father must have been beside himself.'

'When you left he spent the night walking the floor. I could hear him all night.'

'Really?' She stopped and bit her lip. Suddenly I'm the adolescent. Alberto really was his father's son, she reflected, and not just in looks. 'That's between me and your father,' she said repressively.

'Of course. Adult stuff.'

Dervla looked at him suspiciously, unable to rid herself of the idea he was humouring her. The boy looked innocently back at her through eyes that were so like his father's that it was like being pierced by a dull blade.

'You're thirteen. What you did was incredibly dangerous. Anything could have happened,' she said, struggling to impress on him the seriousness of the situation without coming over as the heavy step-parent.

'But it didn't,' he pointed out with another flash of unarguable logic. 'So there's not much point worrying about it, is there?'

'I know your dad can seem a bit unapproachable at times, but if there's a problem you should tell him, Alberto. I think you'd be surprised at how understanding he can be.'

'Oh, don't worry, Dervla, I know I can tell Dad anything and, let's face it, he's the sort of person that you want around in a crisis.'

This piece of worldly wisdom robbed Dervla momentarily of speech. 'Yes, he is,' she admitted finally.

'You look a bit misty, Dervla. Are you all right?' her stepson asked, watching her dab the suspicion of moisture from under her eyes.

'Fine, just a bit of hay fever.' She caught his arm. 'It's just when your father does get here don't whatever you do act as if this is a joke.'

'I won't.'

With that she had to be content as the teenager put on a spurt of speed and shot ahead.

She called his name, breaking into a jog to catch him up.

But she didn't; the teenager with the advantage of longer legs and youth reached the porticoed entrance to the tall Georgian building before she caught up with him.

Dervla stopped at the bottom of the elegant sweep of shallow steps and watched him exchange a few words with the man standing at the open door before disappearing inside.

Run, her inner voice screamed as the man began to walk

down the steps towards her. She might even have responded to the voice had her feet not been nailed to the spot.

'Hello, Gianfranco.' He looked devastatingly handsome in a pale linen shirt open at the neck to reveal smooth golden skin and jeans that clung to his narrow hips and emphasised the length and power of his muscular legs.

The longing rolled over her like a tidal wave as she stared at him.

It did not even occur to her to question his presence here. A year sharing his life had taught her that ingenuity, determination and seemingly limitless financial resources meant that very few things were impossible for Gianfranco.

Compared to some of the things she had witnessed, reaching the London house before them could not have presented much of a challenge to him.

He stopped on the step above her, making the disparity in their heights even more noticeable, but he didn't respond to her polite greeting.

His eyes, dark and intense, remained on her face.

'Alberto's very sorry.'

Dervla saw a flicker of something that looked like amusement in his dark eyes. 'Did he tell you that?'

'Not in so many words, but—'

Gianfranco cut her off with a sharp movement of his hand. '*Dio mio*, I have no wish to discuss my son just now.'

'Not with me, you mean.'

Gianfranco's mouth tightened with frustration.

'It's stupid, really,' Dervla observed, her voice high and shaky. 'But when we got married I was actually nervous about being a step-parent.' She saw the flash of something that might have been shock move in his eyes and laughed again. 'That didn't occur to you? It didn't cross your mind that I was worried I'd mess up and disappoint you.'

'Well, you didn't.'

'Of course I didn't, how could I? You've got the parenting covered. Actually, when you think about it, for someone who refused to be your mistress my present job description is not so very different.

'I've tried hard to fit into your world, Gianfranco, really hard, but it seems to me that, no matter how hard I try, I'll never be good enough.'

A stunned silence followed her quivering emotional outburst.

'Why didn't you tell me you felt that way? I thought you wanted to be part of a family.'

'Haven't you listened to a word I've been saying? I did, I do want to be part of a family, but I'm on the outside looking in where you,' she accused, 'put me.'

He looked genuinely shocked by her claim. 'If that is true it was not my intention.'

'You never do anything accidentally, Gianfranco. You manipulate people.'

'*Per amor di Dio*, you act as though I planned everything…' Releasing a hard laugh, he dragged a hand through his ebony hair and shook his head. 'Since the moment I met you I have been playing catch-up; my life has been about as planned as a forest fire!'

The antagonism drained from Dervla as if someone had released an escape valve. They were just going around in circles. He didn't love her and he wasn't going to change, so what was the point in this?

'Right, fine, well, it doesn't matter any more,' she said dully. 'I'll let you get on with doing your parent things. I'm staying with Sue just now and you've got her number.'

A look of astonishment spread across Gianfranco's lean dark face. For a moment he just stared at her. 'You expect me to stand here and let you walk away…?'

She shrugged, pretending a lack of interest she didn't feel. 'Why not?'

His sable brows twitched into a dark disapproving line. 'What are you talking about? You are my wife, though you seem to have forgotten that.'

Dervla knew she was only his wife on paper. In his heart he would only ever have one wife and it wasn't her. 'I was your wife two days ago,' she observed. 'I didn't see you going out of your way to see if I was all right.'

'So I was meant to follow you?' Eyes smouldering, he stepped down to her level and curved his hands possessively across her narrow ribcage, drawing her towards him until they stood barely an inch apart. The indentation above his aquiline nose deepened as his glance moved across her face.

'You don't look well,' he accused, concern for her fragile appearance making his voice harsh.

'I didn't have much time to make myself presentable.' She made no mention of the fact her brain had gone into meltdown the moment she had heard his voice. 'You said it was urgent so I assumed a trip to the hairdresser's was out of the question.'

The tart retort brought a fleeting smile to his dark eyes. The smile was not there when he said in an intense voice that made her sensitive stomach muscles quiver, 'Your hair always looks beautiful.'

She wanted to lean into him and feel his arms close around her so much it hurt.

Gianfranco's expression was distracted as he brushed a stray curl from her cheek with his knuckles. 'Your skin is so soft!' Silky soft…soft *all over*.

He sucked in air through his flared nostrils as his body reacted strongly to the jolt of lust the stray thought produced.

'I simply meant that you look…' he angled his dark head and allowed his narrowed gaze to travel over the sweet curves of her face '…tired,' he decided, tracing the dark crescents beneath her eyes with the side of his thumb.

Dervla, her thoughts totally occupied with coping with the

ache of longing—he was so damned *close*—had no energy in reserve for prevarication. 'I've not been sleeping.'

Sleeping had become inseparably connected in her mind with the heat of his body, the warm, clean, masculine scent of his silky-textured skin. A sofa and a sleeping bag were just no substitute.

'Neither have I.'

So Alberto had not been wrong about the pacing. 'You haven't?' That was something. 'Why?'

'I was angry with you.'

'*Angry?* I thought you might have missed me…?'

Dervla heard the pleading note in her voice and experienced a stab of self revulsion—where were her pride and self-respect? She was virtually begging.

'Oh, God, this is my fault!' She shook her head, her expression self-recriminatory as she admitted, 'If I'd agreed to be your mistress things wouldn't have got so complicated! I mean, all you ever actually wanted was sex and that's not complicated.'

'It wasn't before I met you,' he intoned grimly. Nothing in his life had been simple since he'd met Dervla.

'Maybe you wish we hadn't got married at all?' A silence followed her words. It stretched and she wanted a hole to open up at her feet and swallow her.

'When you left that way, I was angry, I was concerned, I was…' He stopped, his smouldering dark eyes meshing with Dervla's wide wary gaze.

He vented a frustrated-sounding expletive in his native tongue and pushed both hands into his dark hair before burying his face in his hands.

For what felt like a long time to Dervla he stayed that way. Then his hands fell away and he dragged a hand across his unshaven jaw as his head came up.

The action was so intensely weary that her tender heart took a direct hit. She had been so dazed to find him standing there she had missed the fact that he looked totally exhausted.

More than that, she realised, her troubled stare taking in the telling tension in the skin pulled taut across his chiselled cheekbones and the strain etched into the lines radiating from his deepset eyes, he looked like a man who had been to hell and made the return journey.

Of course he did—his son had gone missing.

The same son he had spoken to for about thirty seconds flat.

Now that did puzzle her; she had fully expected to witness a full-on explosion.

'I did miss you.'

'You *did*?' Her lashes lifted, their eyes connected and her feeble inner defences crumbled. 'I've missed you so much, Gianfranco.'

His eyes flared. 'My bed, had I been able to bring myself to spend any time in it, would have felt as empty as the rest of the house did without you in it,' he told her, his throbbing voice low and intense.

With a cry she launched herself at him like a heat-seeking missile. God, who wants self-respect? Dervla saw the flame of male triumph in his eyes—for a moment it almost resembled relief—before he claimed her mouth.

Then as his arms closed crushingly tight around her, pulling her into him, she didn't care about self-respect. She was where she wanted to be; she was where she belonged.

'You can let me go. I'm not going to disappear,' a much more relaxed-looking Gianfranco said when they finally broke apart.

Dervla shook her head and kept tight hold of his shirt front. 'I've ruined your shirt.'

'I will take it off.'

Dervla could find no fault with this plan.

'Though perhaps somewhere a little less public might be more appropriate.'

Dervla blushed as she realised for the first time they had been locked in a prolonged steamy, passionate embrace in full view of any casual passer-by.

Laughing huskily at her obvious embarrassment, he took her arm to guide her up the steps, but Dervla hung back, shaking her head.

'I have to tell you first, about the baby.'

The poignancy of the moment pierced her. No baby, not ever. She had made her decision and she was calm, but it still hurt.

She was conscious of his stiffening and withdrawing from her at the word. 'I've had time to think about it and you're right.'

He looked wary. 'You don't want a baby?'

Dervla's eyes slid from his. 'I have you and Alberto. If he doesn't need a mother, maybe he needs a friend…?'

'*Dio!*' He clapped a hand to his head and looked at her incredulously. 'Are you trying to shame me?'

Dervla looked at him in incomprehension. 'I don't know what you mean.'

'Do you think I don't know that?'

Mystified by his strange twisted smile, Dervla struggled to read his mood as he framed her face with one brown hand. She closed her eyes as his thumb moved in lazy circles across her cheek.

'Alberto has friends, he has no mother—or rather he didn't.' He dabbed a finger to the moisture as a tear oozed from the corner of her eye. 'Are you sure about this?'

Dervla sniffed and nodded her head. 'Positive. I've decided that I don't want to put myself, us, through all the invasive stuff without even a guarantee it would work.'

I said goodbye to the possibility of having a baby years ago…nothing has really changed, she told herself. She'd survived the knowledge of her infertility for years; surviving without Gianfranco in her life was something she was less sure about.

And she didn't want to find out how she'd cope the hard way.

'And I want this marriage to work.'

'What about in ten or fifteen years' time—will you not look at me and resent the fact I stopped you trying?'

'This is my decision, Gianfranco.'

She struggled to hold his gaze as Gianfranco looked down at her with an unnerving, bone-stripping intensity. She had expected him to look relieved but he didn't.

'You are sure about this.' He was relieved that they could put the entire question behind them for good.

Well, one thing was sure—he need never wonder again if he loved her. A man who loved a woman would never ask her to make the choice he had forced Dervla to make.

'Yes.'

Feeling like a total bastard, he nodded and led her indoors.

Assuming that his first priority would be to tackle his errant son, Dervla was surprised when Gianfranco said Alberto would keep until the next morning and a night spent reflecting on his actions might do him good.

Gianfranco's priorities were quite different. He took her straight up to the privacy of their bedroom suite where he did take off his spoiled shirt and everything else too.

Their lovemaking had a quality to it that had never been there before, an intensity and fierce tenderness that pierced her soul like a dagger and left her with salty tears on her face.

Gianfranco lay on his stomach and she ran her hand down his finely muscled back. '*Dio mio*, I feel as though I've been hit by a train. I mean that in a good way,' he added, rolling onto his back and reaching for her.

She lay there with her head on his heart feeling the reassuring vibration of his heartbeat. Surely a man could not do what he had if he didn't love her just a little bit?

Hugging the reassuring thought to herself, she fell asleep.

CHAPTER ELEVEN

IT WAS dark when Dervla awoke, though not the real dark of the velvet blackness night brought on a Tuscan hilltop.

A darkness that she as a city girl had initially found scary when she had moved into Gianfranco's home in Tuscany. He obviously felt a deep connection to the place and the land. Considering the strength of his feeling, she was surprised that Gianfranco didn't appear to resent the father who had lost it…a poker game, for goodness' sake!

Dervla, who had only ever played the odd hand of whist for buttons, had been utterly stunned when Gianfranco had told her about it, and yet when she had met Fabio Bruni, the quietly spoken charming man had seemed quite normal and not her idea of what constituted someone who had lost a fortune at gaming tables.

When she had commented on this to Gianfranco he had pointed out a compulsive gambling disorder didn't reveal itself in a person's appearance, but in their bank balance and their devastated family life.

'Gianfranco…' She reached out and patted the bed beside her. On finding nothing but a warm indentation, she sat up and called his name again, louder.

This time there was a response. The bathroom door opened and Gianfranco stood framed in the doorway, his tall figure framed by the electric light behind him.

'Hello, sleeping beauty,' he said, striding towards her naked but for the towel precariously slung around his narrow hips and another slung across his shoulders.

She gave a sleepy smile of welcome as he sat down on the edge of the bed and pressed a warm kiss to her lips.

'You're all wet,' she said, grimacing in mock complaint as she ruffled his dripping hair.

'You're all warm,' he retorted huskily as he pulled away the sheet that covered her breasts and inhaled. 'Mmm…you smell good too.'

'What time is it?'

'One-thirty.'

Her eyes widened with shock. 'Seriously…?'

'No, I'm lying…' He rubbed the towel across his dripping dark hair and grinned. 'Of course seriously.'

'I've slept for hours. Why didn't you wake me up? What will people think?' she fretted.

'I've no doubt people will think I have been making wild, passionate and slightly kinky love for the entire night. Which we might have been if I hadn't been comatose too until half an hour ago.'

Mollified by the explanation, she settled back against the pillows. 'What about Alberto?'

'What about Alberto? He hardly requires me to tuck him in.'

'Don't worry too much about him, Gianfranco,' she advised, sure he was a lot more worried than he was letting on about his son's escapade. 'I'm sure there's some perfectly simple explanation.'

'I'm sure there is.'

'And, Gianfranco, don't be too tough. Try and remember what it is to be a young boy with hormones.'

'I think I can just about recall what a hormone feels like.' He could also recall what she felt like in his arms.

'Do you think,' she mused, her eyes narrowing as she considered the problem, 'it could be about the exams he has coming up? A lot of people suffer badly from exam nerves. I did.' She glanced at her husband, sure he had never felt a twinge of nerves in an exam room in his life. 'And you're a really hard act for any boy to follow. Perhaps he feels intimidated…?' She made the suggestion tentatively.

'I somehow doubt that,' Gianfranco said drily. 'As for matching my academic achievements, that should not be difficult. I have none.'

'How do you mean you have none?'

'I didn't actually take any exams.'

'None?'

He had tilted his dark head in acknowledgment of her question, looking amused by her astonishment.

'I was within a few months of taking my exams when I was asked to leave school.'

'You were expelled?'

'Nothing so glamorous.' He trailed a finger along her cheek and laughed.

Dervla caught his hand raised it to her lips and didn't smile back, then with a sigh rubbed her cheek into his palm. She heard his sharp intake of breath and saw his eyes darken dramatically. For a second their eyes clung, then his smouldering gaze dropped with slow deliberation to her lips.

She felt light-headed with lust as the tightening low in her pelvis intensified, but she dug into her reserves of control and, instead of leaning into him when he reached to drag her to him, she shuffled on her bottom down the silken sheet.

'Why did you leave, then?' He never spoke of his past and she couldn't let this opportunity pass.

He gave a resigned shrug. 'You are imagining some mystery. There is none.' He picked up a pillow and tucked it in behind his head and leaned back.

Dervla dragged her eyes upwards from the ripple of the slabs of hard muscle in his flat golden abdomen.

Her expression became indignant when she saw the smug glitter of amusement in his eyes as he observed her obvious struggle.

'All right, you're totally irresistible,' she confirmed crossly, 'but it might make my life easier if you wore a stitch of clothing.'

His grin deepened as he quirked a dark brow. 'I have no body issue.'

'You're an exhibitionist,' she accused, tacking on before she became fatally distracted, 'So why did you leave school?'

'My fees weren't paid.'

Her eyes widened. 'So they asked you to leave? Oh, that's terrible.' She was indignant on his behalf. 'Callous!' she added in disgust at the institution that had put profit before the welfare of a gifted pupil.

'Actually over the years they had been pretty patient. The bursar would drop a tactful word in my ear and mention that the payment was a little late. There was usually a painting or a piece of jewellery to sell and then,' he said with a careless shrug, 'there wasn't.

'Don't look so tragic, *cara mia*. Formal education was not for me; it was too…' his broad shoulder lifted expressively as he explained '…too confining. They actually did me a favour. Within a month of being chucked out I had started the dot-com company, which I sold before the bubble burst, and the rest, as they say, is history.'

'Don't you mind that your father acts as though the palazzo is still his when he comes to stay?' In reality Gianfranco had paid a whacking premium to save the palazzo and estate from a developer when he had restored the family fortunes.

'It is a matter of pride. What is the point in rubbing salt in the wound? Besides, he is a reformed man these days, as much as any compulsive gambler can be reformed.'

'Well, I think you're an incredibly generous man,' she said impulsively. 'Considering what he put your mother and you through.'

'We all have our weaknesses, Dervla.'

She regarded him doubtfully. 'Even you?'

'Even me,' he confirmed.

'I don't believe you.'

'You should. My weakness is a redheaded witch who barely reaches my shoulder.' And he was so deeply under her spell he no longer even wanted to escape.

She stared, amazed by the declaration. 'I think that's a compliment…?'

He shrugged and threw aside the towel around his neck. 'I don't know about that, but it's the truth. About that warmth, *cara mia*—do you feel like sharing it with me?'

She threw him a look that was almost shy and folded back the covers beside her. 'I'd enjoy warming you up.'

She did.

The next time Dervla woke it was light and the bed beside her was empty and cold. Her smile of sleepy contentment changed to a frown.

Lifting herself on one elbow, she was about to call Gianfranco's name when she caught sight of the dial on the clock on the nightstand. Her eyes widened; it was lunchtime.

She swung her legs over the side and brushed back the tangled skein of hair from her brow and headed for the shower.

Gianfranco should have woken her.

She told him the same thing when she went downstairs and found him in the kitchen.

'I did try.' He placed one hand on her denim-covered bottom and smoothed the still-wet curls back from her cheek with the other. 'I tried kissing you awake, but you just rolled over and snuggled down like a sleepy kitten.'

His lean face was close and Dervla leaned into him with a sigh and turned her face up to his. 'It couldn't have been much of a kiss,' she teased.

He bared his teeth in a lazy and impossibly sexy smile and without warning grabbed her and, framing her face between his hands, covered her mouth with his.

'Now that,' she admitted, raising a not quite steady hand to her tingling lips as she struggled to catch her breath, 'would have woken me.'

'I tell you, it didn't, and I would have stayed around and kept you company, but I had some calls to make.'

She gave a sceptical snort. 'You never stay in bed.' It was true Gianfranco was not only an early riser, awake literally with the birds each day, but he was one of those rare people who could get by on a couple of hours' sleep. The only time she had known him stay in bed was on their honeymoon in the secluded clifftop Corsican villa, when they had virtually camped in the four-poster in the fairy-tale turret bedroom.

When she had at one point during the week suggested to Gianfranco—without very much enthusiasm, it had to be admitted—that they really should get dressed and explore the beautiful area, he had paused in the act of pushing open the full-length windows that allowed the sound of waves far below to fill the room and looked at her, his expression baffled.

'Why?'

'Because what do I say when people ask me what the island was like?'

'Recommend a good guidebook.'

'Don't be flippant. I'm serious.'

'You are totally ridiculous,' he corrected firmly. 'In case you have forgotten, this is our honeymoon, *cara*, and if these people whose opinion concerns you have any tact at all they will not ask such questions.'

'What are you thinking about?' Gianfranco asked now. 'You have a far-away look in your eyes.'

'I was far away,' she admitted. 'In Corsica.'

His eyes darkened. 'Then you know that I do stay in bed if I have the right encouragement. Do you feel,' he asked, lifting a curl off her cheek, 'like supplying that encouragement?'

Thinking of her last-minute appointment at the fertility clinic, her eyes fell from his. 'I'd like to, but I've got an appointment…'

Controlling his dissatisfaction with her response with difficulty, he let his hand fall away. 'Where are you going?'

Dervla leant forward to pour herself some coffee from the pot on the table, allowing her hair to fall forward to partially conceal her face from his view. 'I've got a dental appointment. I lost a filling.'

She met his eyes nervously. The rehearsed lie sounded so false to her that she fully expected him to pounce on the deceit.

Instead Gianfranco looked immediately concerned. 'Why didn't you say, *cara*? Are you in pain?'

'No, it's not too bad, just a bit sensitive with hot and cold,' she lied, feeling guiltier than ever.

'Hold on, I will come with you.'

'No…no!' With a smile she moderated her tone and added, 'That is, I really think you should take the opportunity to have a proper talk with Alberto.' She lowered her voice as her glance slid in the direction of the boy at the breakfast table, his eyes nodding, his head in tune with the music being fed to him via earphones.

'I mean, we still don't know why he ran away that way.' Her concern about this did not have to be feigned. 'And it might be easier for him to talk if I'm not here.' Dervla's eyes dropped. 'You were right—Alberto might resent my interfering.'

'You couldn't make Alberto resent you if you tried. I was wrong.' He looked at her with an expression she found hard to interpret. 'You are not an interloper in this family, Dervla, you are a fully paid-up member. You do not need to excuse yourself to give us time alone.'

Dervla's throat closed over with emotion. So he hadn't been paying lip service yesterday; he had actually meant what he said. God, if she felt guilty for lying to him before, she felt positively wretched about it now!

After today she promised herself they would have no more secrets.

The doctor listened politely when she explained that, having discussed the matter with her husband, they had decided not to take part in the clinical trial.

'Actually, Mrs Bruni, I have to tell you that you are not actually a candidate for the trial.'

Dervla received the news in shocked silence.

'So there never was a chance that I might become pregnant?'

Her shoulders slumped. She wasn't sure if she felt relieved or disappointed…maybe both…?

It was ironic, all that heart-searching, and for what?

'It seems quite clear to me that you already are pregnant, Mrs Bruni.'

CHAPTER TWELVE

DERVLA was vaguely aware of being guided into a chair. She stared at the glass of water in her hand and had no recollection of how it got there.

The buzzing in her ears lessened slightly as she lifted her eyes to the doctor who hovered over her. 'Sorry about that,' she apologised with a strained laugh. 'But I thought for a second there that you said I was pregnant.'

'Had you no suspicion?'

'*Suspicion?*' she echoed, thinking violent mood swings, a sudden aversion to coffee, tender breasts. 'How could I have a suspicion?' she demanded shrilly.

The signs had been there, but she hadn't been looking... Why would she be looking?

'You said yourself that for me to conceive naturally would take a miracle,' she protested. 'And I'd have known... Women do, don't they?' The ones she spoke to seemed to.

'It is not uncommon for a woman not to realise she's pregnant until the pregnancy is quite well advanced, and miracles, even in this cynical world, are not nearly as rare as you might imagine. In my job I see miracles every day, birth itself is a miracle.'

Dervla, her eyes wide in Bambi-like shock, released a long shuddering sigh as her hands curved in an instinctively protective gesture across her stomach. She lifted a hand to cover her mouth and realised that she was shaking hard.

She had come here to close the door on her last chance to ever have her own baby and he was telling her that she was going to have a baby. She shook her head, still unable to fully believe she wasn't asleep and dreaming.

'You haven't got my results mixed up with someone else's?'

'*Quite* sure.' The doctor seemed more amused than offended by her suspicious question. 'You are pregnant.'

'Oh, my God!' What was Gianfranco going to say? She pushed away the thought. It was hard enough for her just to get her head around the basic facts without tackling that issue.

'How pregnant?' Her thoughts raced. How long had she been walking around oblivious to the life growing within her? How was it possible for her not to have known?

'From the physical examination I'd say twelve weeks, but will be able to tell you more accurately after the scan.'

My baby… For the first time she allowed herself to believe and joy seeped through her. 'I'm having a scan?' If she saw her own baby it might seem more real and less like a dream. 'When?'

'Right now, if you would like.'

'I'd like.'

The doctor laughed at her fervent affirmation and left the room to make the necessary arrangements.

Dervla couldn't tear her fascinated eyes off the screen. 'It really is a baby,' she whispered, absently wiping the moisture from her face with the back of her hand. 'A miracle,' she added huskily. 'Is he all right? There's nothing…?'

'Your baby is perfect and according to the measurements about…yes, you're fourteen weeks along.'

'I really can't take this in. I'm sure I should be asking questions.' She shook her head, sniffed and admitted huskily, 'I just don't know…I never thought I'd be in this situation…' Her voice cracked as she fought back a teary sob.

The doctor smiled and handed her a tissue. 'I'd be glad to answer any questions. Why don't you make an appointment to come back with your husband when things have sunk in? I'm sure he'd like to be involved.'

Dervla, who was equally sure he wouldn't, felt a shaft of searing pain so sharp she gasped.

'You're really kind. Thank you very much.'

She left the clinic and, still in a daze, took a detour through the park. She walked aimlessly, her mind in a total whirl, her emotional state fluctuating wildly between euphoria and fear.

It still didn't feel real.

How could it?

Having a baby was not something she had allowed herself to even dream about until recently. And she had made a conscious choice to give up on that dream. Taken the decision not to pursue it, because doing so would have destroyed her marriage.

She wanted Gianfranco's child and she wanted Gianfranco. She couldn't have both.

She sat down heavily on a bench and buried her face in her hands.

When she lifted her face it was pale but determined. Why couldn't she have both? Gianfranco had seemed set against the baby idea, but part of that had been his lack of enthusiasm—one she was sure many men shared—for the invasive nature of medical intervention.

He had a son, he was great with kids. He'd be great with *their* kid once he got used to the idea. An image flickered across her mind and for an instant she saw Gianfranco's face, his exact expression when he had told her he didn't want more children, *ever*.

She gritted her teeth and pushed the image away. That was then, this was now. Things had changed; he'd have to.

This was not the moment for negative thoughts. Think straight, Dervla, she told herself. Think straight! It sounded so easy. She shook her head to clear her brain. Trying to link two thoughts together was like wading through treacle.

This wasn't the sort of thing you could just drop on him, not yet. You couldn't tell a man one night you had given up on the idea of babies, then turn up the next morning and casually drop, 'I'm pregnant,' into the conversation.

It would be sensible to drop a few hints, though she was a bit vague on what form those hints might take.

He just needed time and he'd come around. Even in her present state of denial this rationalisation was too much for her inner voice to take in silence.

Because Gianfranco is so malleable?

She inhaled, took a deep breath and squared her shoulders and thought, No, because he has to.

Because he has to want this baby as much as I do.

They had been back a week and life was as near to perfect as Dervla could imagine.

It would have been perfect but for her secret. It hung over her head like the proverbial sword swinging precariously by a thread. Dervla continued to duck it and the truth.

She had to tell Gianfranco she was pregnant. It wasn't as if it was going to go away and she didn't want it to. She had no choice and time was running out; it wouldn't be long before she was showing.

Her body had already undergone some subtle changes courtesy of the small life growing within her—fascinating changes. Changes that seemed so dramatic to Dervla that she couldn't believe Gianfranco hadn't noticed. But beyond an approving observation concerning her increased bra size—he had totally misinterpreted her blushing response to his remarks— he appeared oblivious.

It was becoming increasingly obvious that the perfect moment she had been waiting for, somewhere along the lines of Gianfranco seeing a baby in a pram and saying wistfully, 'Life would be perfect if we could have our own child,' giving her the opportunity to turn around and say, 'Well, actually, we have,' simply wasn't going to happen outside her fantasies. And even in them it had never really been very convincing!

It might actually turn out that she was stressing, giving herself nightmares, for nothing. There was no reason to assume he was going to hate the idea—and very possibly her. When faced with the reality of a baby Gianfranco might have a massive change of heart; he might embrace the idea and be as blown away as she was.

Then again he might not.

This was a possibility she had to prepare herself for, but couldn't.

Every time she tried to predict his reaction she broke out in a cold sweat. There was only one way to find out.

She had to tell him.

How bad could it be? Surely no worse than walking around weighed down by this permanent feeling of guilt? Nothing could be worse than that, except possibly having your husband hate you and your marriage destroyed…

It wasn't meant to be this way.

She kept remembering the look on Kate's face when she had told her about the pregnancy.

'I've never thought of myself as the maternal type,' the other girl had confided ruefully. 'So I never expected to feel this way, and when I told Angelo he cried…he really cried. You know, I didn't think we could get any closer but I was wrong. This baby has brought us even closer.'

It seemed so unfair!

Telling the man you loved that you were carrying his child was meant to be one of life's great moments.

* * *

But then having spent her morning in the children's hospice Dervla knew only too well that fair was something life simply wasn't.

If anything was guaranteed to put life and your own troubles in perspective, it was spending a morning with the children and parents in this place.

People visited here for the first time expecting to find it depressing, but left speaking of an uplifting, life-affirming experience after meeting the brave patients.

Certainly Dervla left that morning with a new sense of purpose. Things were clearer in her head than they had been for weeks.

I will tell Gianfranco this evening, she resolved as she opened the car door.

She was about to drive away when a smiling Sister Agnes, one of the several nuns who worked at the hospice, tapped on the window.

Dervla immediately rolled it down.

'Hello, Sister, is there something I can do for you?' she asked, assuming the nun had had a thought about the hospice-at-home nursing service that had been top of the agenda.

The meeting had been extremely productive, which was good because it helped, Dervla reflected, if one thing in a person's life was going according to plan!

'No, no, it's not that. I just wanted a little private word.'

Dervla smiled. 'Of course.' She reached out to switch off the engine but the diminutive sister forestalled her, reaching through the window and patting her hand.

'No, dear, I won't keep you. I just wanted to say how happy I am for you,' the smiling nun explained in the Irish lilt that she hadn't lost even after twenty years in Italy.

Dervla gave a bemused little shake of her head. 'I'm sorry, I don't…'

'You'll make a lovely mother, and that man of yours—well, you've got a good one there, as I'm sure you know, my dear.'

Dervla looked at her with blank astonishment, a hand going

involuntarily to her stomach as she felt the colour climb to her cheeks. 'How…how…?'

'No, you don't show,' she soothed. 'My mother was the same. She always knew before the doctor. Just a little gift I've inherited.'

'Right, well, thank you, but we've not actually—'

The nun raised a finger to her lips. 'Mum's the word,' she promised with a twinkle. 'If you'll pardon the pun.'

Dervla, who was too flustered to even register the pun, gave a vague smile. 'I'll see you soon, Sister,' she promised.

The encounter with the nun brought home with a vengeance the growing urgency of telling Gianfranco about the baby. If he found out from anyone but her she could only imagine how he would react—and that thought made her shudder.

A person who always faced problems head-on, he would not begin to understand why she had delayed telling him.

Tonight it was a charity dinner, tomorrow she would no doubt discover some other perfectly legitimate reason why it wasn't the right time to tell Gianfranco, so why wait?

'Yes, definitely tonight,' she said, glancing at the waving nun in the rear-view mirror

She wouldn't have waited that long if she hadn't already arranged to have lunch with Carla. She would have driven straight to Gianfranco's Florence office, but she had already put off the older woman twice since she got home.

Home—it did feel like home more than any other place she had ever known. But, cliché or not, she knew that any place Gianfranco was would feel like home.

What she had was worth fighting for and if she had to beat Gianfranco over the head with a stick to make him realise that a baby was cause for celebration she would do just that!

Carla was sitting in the restaurant sipping a mineral water when Dervla arrived.

'I'm sorry I'm late,' she said as the other woman rose and

kissed her on both cheeks. Acutely sensitive to smells of late, she felt a wave of nausea as she was engulfed by a cloud of the woman's heavy perfume.

'Don't you look lovely?' Carla said as Dervla took her seat and told the waiter a mineral water would be fine for her. 'And such comfortable shoes,' the older woman admired. 'My.' She sighed. 'How I wish I wasn't such a slave to fashion. Now before we start let me just say that I have told everyone it's just a silly rumour.'

Dervla put down the menu. 'What's a silly rumour?'

'When you went away like that there was some talk, but I told—'

'There was talk?' Dervla was dismayed. She had not imagined her brief flight would have attracted attention and the idea of being the target of gossip dismayed her.

'Talk of divorce, but don't worry, I told them all couples argue and Gianfranco would never cheat.'

'Of course he wouldn't!'

'Don't worry, I am totally discreet.'

'There's nothing to be discreet about.'

'That is what I told them.' Carla gave a cheery smile and applied herself to the menu. 'I said just look how happy they are and remember how worried we were for Gianfranco when Sara died. It was such a terrible time. If it wasn't for Alberto needing him there were some people who even suggested he might do something silly…' She let her voice trail away as she threw Dervla a significant look.

'Never!' Dervla's protest was drawn straight from the heart.

Gianfranco was not a quitter; no matter how tough the going got he would never take the easy way out.

The other woman, looking visibly disconcerted by Dervla's vehemence, quickly agreed. 'I'm sure you're right. The lobster here is very good, I believe.'

Dervla passed on the lobster in a rich sauce and chose the

lightest thing she could see on the menu. Even so she had barely begun to push her food around the table when she had to dive into the powder room.

Dervla always felt unkempt and underdressed when she was around this immaculately groomed woman, but returning to the table a short while later she felt the comparison even more acutely.

A brief glance in the mirror after she had splashed her face with water had shown that in the process what little make-up she had been wearing had gone.

Carla stared as she sat down.

'You're pregnant, aren't you?'

Dervla was too startled and dismayed at having her secret uncovered for the second time that day to wonder at the harshness in the older woman's voice.

'Yes, I am.'

The older woman's thin lips curved into a stiff smile. 'Congratulations.'

'Thank you. I'd be grateful if you didn't say anything to anyone just yet. It isn't...it isn't public yet.' It isn't even private.

'Very wise, so much can happen in the early days. I understand that quite a large proportion of pregnancies end in—'

Dervla's voice, high and shrill, cut across her. 'No! My baby is fine,' she blurted, her pale face flooding with colour.

Carla raised a thin brow. 'Of course not. I didn't mean to suggest anything would happen; I was just agreeing with your decision not to go public this early.'

'Actually not that early.'

'I won't breathe a word. Gianfranco must be delighted.'

Dervla felt the guilty blush travel up her neck. 'Well, actually, I haven't told him yet.'

'Really?'

'You must think it odd.'

'I'm sure you have your reasons.' She tipped her head back

and smiled, revealing her even teeth white against her crimson lips. 'But don't worry, I won't say a word.'

Two hours later Carla was sitting in the pavement café opposite the rear entrance to the Bruni Building—the entrance Gianfranco used.

As she saw Gianfranco's tall figure emerge through the door she glanced quickly at her reflection in her compact mirror, smiling when she liked what she saw, and slid it back into her bag.

Taking the direct route across the street, she was able to artfully collide with Gianfranco before he reached his parked car.

'I'm sorry. Are you all right?' Gianfranco's hand went automatically out to steady the female who had barrelled into him. One brow lifted when he identified the dark-haired woman. 'Carla, you're in a hurry.'

'I am running a bit late,' she admitted, clicking her tongue as she glanced down at the designer bags spilling their contents on the pavement.

'Been shopping?'

It occurred to Gianfranco that there was very little else in this woman's life. Of course her day might involve something beyond shopping—beauty parlours, manicurists and being seen in the right places—but if it did she never mentioned it.

Dervla would be bored stiff, he realised, unable to imagine his wife being content with such a hedonistic, shallow existence, although, he thought, his forehead creasing into a concerned frown, she took it too far sometimes.

While he was immensely proud of what she had achieved getting the hospice project up and running in such a short space of time, he worried that she took too much on. He knew that a lot of people assumed that he had been the driving force behind the scheme.

Nothing could be farther from the truth, and anyone that suggested such a thing to him was swiftly disabused, but Dervla herself didn't seem concerned about recognition of her hard work.

It seemed to him sometimes that she didn't understand the meaning of delegation, or for that matter the word no—someone asked her to do something and she said yes without considering how thin she was spreading herself.

When he had spoken to her about it she had not appeared to treat his comments seriously.

'I like to keep busy, and anyway you're one to talk. When was the last time you lay on your back in the grass and just watched the clouds?'

'Why would I do that?'

When Dervla stopped laughing she lifted her slender shoulders and said, 'Point proven, I think. You thrive on pressure, Gianfranco.'

'I know my limitations.'

'Now that is so not true it isn't even funny.'

He had let the subject drop, but that had been a mistake. The line etched between his eyes deepened as he remembered how pale and drawn she had looked that morning when he'd left.

He wasn't about to let her drive herself into the ground, but he knew that the moment his back was turned she'd be doing something stupid again.

The only solution that immediately presented itself was not turning his back so often. Maybe he should take some of his own advice—given the right company he might even learn to see some purpose to watching clouds.

'Ouch!'

The high-pitched shriek recalled Gianfranco to his surroundings and the woman who was trying to retrieve her shopping from the pavement. Her efforts were considerably hampered by a skin-tight pencil skirt and four-inch heels.

Gianfranco dropped down. 'Let me.' The first thing he picked up was a tiny baby sleepsuit.

With a laugh Carla snatched it from his hand. 'You'll just have to pretend you haven't seen it when Dervla unwraps it.' Brushing down her skirt, she rose to her feet and held the tiny garment at arm's length. 'Do you think Dervla will like it?' She stopped as an idea seemed to occur to her. 'Oh, tell me she hasn't already bought one like this?'

Gianfranco looked at the sleepsuit and replied with some confidence, 'I'm almost a hundred per cent sure she hasn't.'

It was about the only thing he felt confident about at that moment.

Carla gave an exaggerated sigh of relief. 'Well, thank goodness for that. I nearly got this delicious little cardigan, but then I thought is cashmere really practical for a baby? I just couldn't resist it when I saw it,' she babbled on. 'The darling little rabbit ears are so cute.' She intercepted his frozen look and laughed again—the tinkling artificial sound was really beginning to grate on him. 'Sorry, I'm gushing, but you're going to have to get used to that,' she teased.

Gianfranco put the rest of the parcels in the bags and rose slowly to his feet.

'Thank you,' Carla said, planting a kiss on his cheek as she took the bags. 'You must be so excited.' Appearing not to notice the fact he was standing like a block of wood, she kissed him again before tottering on her four-inch heels towards the café-bar opposite.

CHAPTER THIRTEEN

THERE had to be some sort of mistake.

Dervla couldn't have a baby. Why would Carla assume she was?

Gianfranco saw her pale face, the worrying tiredness, early visits to the bathroom.

Dio mio! He sucked in a deep breath through flared nostrils and, his expression frozen, wrenched open the car door.

Placing her evening gown, a satiny creation in pale green with a tight bodice—too tight right now—and flowing skirt on the bed, Dervla, wearing her pink lace-trimmed strapless bra and matching pants, sat in front of her dressing-table mirror.

The diamond necklace she had already fastened around her neck glittered against her smooth skin as she reached for the matching diamond studs. The set had been a gift from Gianfranco just after they returned home and he had specifically requested she wear them tonight.

A dreamy smile played across her lips as, holding the studs to her ears, she turned her head to see the effect. Her smile faded as it occurred to her that the only thing he might request of her after tonight was that she pack a bag and leave.

Not that he would do that, of course—he had a strong sense

of duty—but he might wish he could, which was in some ways worse.

Once she told him she would no longer have the luxury of fantasising, taking refuge in illogical romanticism and picturing him getting misty eyes and realising that fatherhood was after all exactly what he wanted.

She would have to live with the uncomfortable reality of what was happening.

Every time she speculated on his reaction she felt sick. Not that there was much doubt in her mind during rational moments about his reaction—the choice was between rage and revulsion.

Her only hope was that he would eventually warm to the idea.

She was telling herself that this would happen when a flicker of movement in the periphery of the mirror made her turn her head.

Gianfranco was standing there, his long, lean length propped against the door frame of the dressing room, his expression not encouraging her to believe he would ever warm to anything ever again.

Her stomach sank. 'You know.'

He inhaled a deep breath and levered himself off the door. 'Then it is true?' he said harshly.

'How—?'

His dismissed her question with a jerk of his head. 'That is not important.'

'Sit down,' she pleaded. 'I can't talk to you while you're—'

'Talk!' He spat out the word in disgust. 'I think the time for talking has come and gone.'

'I know I should have told you,' she admitted, shamefaced.

'Told me what—a pack of lies?'

She recoiled from the hostility in his voice. 'I have never lied to you.' A few omissions concerning the subject of love. 'Except about the dental appointment.'

He looked at her blankly. 'Dental appointment?'

'The day after I brought Alberto home.'

The colour receded further from his face. 'You knew then?'

She nodded. 'It came as an enormous shock to me. I didn't even suspect and—'

'It came as an enormous shock to you. *Madre di Dio!* What do you think it came as to me? You told me you could not have children. How many other lies,' he wondered bitterly, 'have you told me?'

'You…!' She felt her anger stir; this wasn't fair. Why couldn't he see that this was a good thing? See that a baby was a blessing? 'This isn't all about you. This isn't a conspiracy, or a devious plan. I was told that the chances of me ever becoming pregnant naturally or, for that matter, any way were remote bordering on impossible! I believed it.'

'So this is a miracle conception?'

His sneer sent a rush of anger through her body. 'As far as I am concerned, yes, it is.'

The quiet dignity of her retort seemed to take him momentarily aback. 'You want this child?'

'Our child,' she corrected quietly.

'I have no say in the matter, then?'

Dervla went icy cold. 'You're suggesting I have an abortion?'

He looked shocked by the suggestion, but Dervla was too angry to notice. 'What? *No!* Of course I'm not—'

'But you wouldn't shed any tears if I lost the baby. God, but you're so selfish. I don't know why I didn't see it before,' she said, staring at him with disillusion.

He responded to her angry accusation with a stony stare.

'I'm damned if you'll make me feel as though I've done something I should be ashamed of,' she declared proudly. Fumbling with the clasp of the necklace, suddenly desperate to remove his gift, she began to cry in frustration. 'Damn this thing, it won't come off!' she sniffed, tugging at the wretched thing until it left a red mark on her fair skin.

'*Dio mio*, stop it—you'll hurt yourself,' he said, removing her hands forcibly from her throat.

Dervla held herself rigid as his fingers brushed her throat, deeply ashamed of the stab of desire that pierced her at his touch.

'There,' he said, dropping the necklace into her palm.

'I got pregnant accidentally—and, in case you've forgotten, not without some assistance. I didn't rob a bank!' She bit her trembling lower lip and turned her head away, adding huskily, 'Although from the way you're acting you'd probably prefer that!'

'You told me you couldn't have children.' If he had known he could have used protection and kept her safe.

Teeth clenched, she matched his glare. 'That's what I was told.' She flung up her hands. 'Or do you think I invented my entire medical history for some sinister motive of my own? I didn't plan for this to happen, but I'm damned glad it did.

'It's something I never thought could happen to me, but it did, and you may sneer but it is a miracle and I don't care what you say or think—I intend to be happy about it,' she declared, before bursting into breathless tears.

He looked on helplessly as she wept. Her accusations echoed around his head. He wanted to tell her how wrong she was, but he couldn't do so without revealing his guilt and his fear.

How could he explain that for him pregnancy did not equate with happiness? In his mind it was inextricably linked with illness and danger. He had no right to infect her with his fear, a fear that would dog every day of her pregnancy.

'I'm sorry, Dervla, I'm sorry I can't feel about this the way you want me to.'

She lifted her tear-drenched eyes to his face. She felt emotionally exhausted and drained; just speaking was an effort. 'This is our baby,' she said, pressing a hand to her stomach.

He nodded. 'I know. It was a shock.'

'And you hid it so well.'

'We'll work something out.' If anything happened to her

because of this he would never be able to live with himself. He would never be able to live without her, because—and how had he pretended it wasn't so this long?—he loved her.

'There's nothing to work out. I'm having a baby and if you by look or glance ever make him or her feel unwanted I will never, ever forgive you.'

He went into his study, poured himself a brandy, then, after looking at the glass, emptied the contents into a pot plant.

Along with gambling, his father had drunk to excess when he had a problem—usually his latest gambling debt. He was not a role model that Gianfranco had ever felt the urge to emulate, so why start now? He didn't need to find anaesthesia in a bottle.

So he'd been a loser on the love-marriage lottery once; it didn't mean he had to allow history to repeat itself.

He should celebrate that he had such a wonderful wife—one he could love?

He could sit around being a hypochondriac by proxy, imagining all sorts of nightmare scenarios, or he could make sure that Dervla and their baby stayed safe.

He was still planning his strategy when Dervla entered without knocking. She was wearing a long nightdress that was transparent in the lamplight. On another occasion he might have supposed she had chosen it deliberately to seduce him, but that was clearly not the case now.

She looked from him to the open bottle on the table. 'Have you been drinking?'

'No, I changed my mind.'

'Are you coming to bed?'

'Would I be welcome?'

Her eyes slid from his and she shrugged.

'In the morning I will arrange a nurse—someone to live in— and I will transfer your care to doctors here. Angelo will know the best ones.'

'That's not necessary.' But it clearly was for him. She realised that by surrounding her with professional carers he would be able to distance himself.

Recognising his motives filled her with a profound sadness. She had really thought, even after this evening, that maybe he might thaw a little to the idea.

CHAPTER FOURTEEN

'DERVLA!'

Gianfranco wondered at the sound of heels on the marble floor of the hallway in response to his call. Dervla rarely wore shoes in the house at the moment; it was her last month of her pregnancy and her feet had begun to swell.

An alarming development for him at least, but the consultant, a professor no less, had reassured him on the subject. 'No, your wife definitely does not have pre-eclampsia. The symptom in isolation is not dangerous.'

'Gianfranco!'

He turned and saw not his wife but Carla. His disappointment was too intense for him to disguise it.

'Carla.' His dark eyes went beyond her. 'Where is Dervla?'

The brunette, one hand pressed flat on her narrow chest, placed the other on his arm. 'I'm sorry, Gianfranco—'

Her dramatic pause only succeeded in irritating him; so did the smell of the heavy perfume she seemed to have bathed in. 'I'm afraid she has gone—again.'

He bared his teeth in an angry smile. Afraid? Dervla would be damn afraid when he caught up with her—only she wouldn't, would she? She'd just stick out her chin and glare at him with the 'to hell with you' expression in her glorious green eyes. Or look all fragile and vulnerable and make him feel like a total bastard.

Either way, she'd make him want to kiss her, and not doing so these last months was wearing him down like a war of attrition. One day soon he was going to implode or spontaneously combust—something fatal and messy!

When, he wondered bleakly, was she going to forgive him? And stop keeping him at arm's length?

And what was she doing gallivanting around in her condition with a storm coming? And it was—he could feel it in the sticky thickness of the air.

'Gone where?' His nostrils wrinkled in distaste as Carla swayed closer. Dervla's perfume, when she did wear one, was something subtle and elusive. Thinking about it sent a stab of desire through his body.

Oh, well, he'd lost control of his mind so why not his body too? He hated feeling powerless, but actually he was almost getting used to it.

Frustration made his stomach muscles clench. 'Dervla.' Sometimes he felt an overpowering urge to simply say her name.

Unaware that Carla had withdrawn her hand sharply from his sleeve, or that she was staring at him, barely even conscious of her presence, he dragged a brown hand across his forehead and strode across to the window. The trees that lined the long driveway were swaying in a wind that was a gentle breeze compared to what was to come later.

Summer storms could be ferocious, elemental here in the hills, and it was the thought of Dervla experiencing her first one alone that had made him cancel his afternoon meetings and drive straight back home while he still could.

'Did she say when she'd be back?' He flicked back the cuff of his shirt and squinted down at his watch. He'd give her ten minutes; if she hadn't returned by then he'd go and get her.

'Let me get you a drink,' Carla purred compassionately.

He turned to see the tall woman glide with a lot of overdone hip-swaying to the cabinet.

'I don't want a drink,' he said shortly as she pulled out two glasses and a bottle. 'I want to know when my wife said she'd be back.'

'She won't be coming back, Gianfranco.'

Gianfranco looked at her, eyes narrowed, expression closed, and barked in a voice that anyone in the business community who had tried to get the better of him would have instantly recognized, 'Where the hell is my wife?'

Carla's misty smile faded as she took an involuntary step backwards. The fury blazing in Gianfranco's eyes was meant for her... This wasn't the way this was meant to be going. 'That's what I'm trying to tell you, Gianfranco.' Struggling to regain her composure, she ran her tongue across her dry lips. 'She has left.' And I am here to offer you comfort.

Gianfranco looked at her for a moment, then smiled.

The smile made Carla wonder for the first time if she had miscalculated. He did not look like a man who needed comfort; he looked like a man capable of doing anything to get what he wanted. It was beginning to dawn on her that he already had what he wanted and he'd do whatever it took to get it back.

'I know you're lying, Carla.' He noted her pallor but felt no sympathy. One thing he knew with total certainty was that Dervla would not leave him without a word.

And if she has, the voice in his head said, whose fault would it be? If you'd had the backbone to stop pretending, even to yourself, and come clean with her.

You need someone.

The idea of spending your life without that someone is the worst nightmare you ever dreamt existed.

He loved her. If souls were born searching, his had been born searching for Dervla's. The thing he had claimed to despise most had happened to him. Saying something did not exist didn't make it go away, it just left you less prepared and in denial when it caught hold of you.

And it had caught hold of him hard.

He was no longer the owner of his heart. It now belonged to Dervla.

'What I don't know is why. But I will,' he promised softly. 'Before you leave here I will know, and, in case you are in any doubt, yes, that was a threat.'

Carla stared at Gianfranco as though she had never seen him before. Her face pale under her perfectly applied make-up, she plucked nervously at the string of pearls around her neck. 'You're upset, Gianfranco.'

Gianfranco struggled with the growing desire to shake the truth out of her bony carcass. 'And I'm about to get even more upset if you don't stop lying to me.'

'I'm not lying. She's left you before,' she reminded him shrilly. 'Why wouldn't she do it again? It was inevitable really, and probably for the best in the long run.' Her expression settled into an ugly, malicious sneer as she added, 'She was never one of us.' Her face softened into an indulgent smile as she waved her finger at him and reproached, 'You have to admit, Gianfranco, you have terrible taste in women. First the barmaid, then *this* one. Do you ever wonder how different life would be if you'd married me as we planned?'

'Planned?'

'When I was twenty you said you wanted to marry me.'

It took him a second to realise that she was referring to the adolescent joke…only she wasn't joking. 'I was sixteen.' The woman was clearly either drunk or delusional.

'And so handsome. Don't look like that, Gianfranco. I understand that a man like you needs a wife who appreciates him, someone who understands that a man in your position needs support, not criticism.'

As he listened to her speak the knot of fear in Gianfranco's belly tightened. His pregnant wife was missing and he was becoming more convinced with each passing second that this madwoman had something to do with it.

An insane woman was a guest in his house!

'Someone who would agree with everything I say, you mean? *Dio!*' He snorted, his soft voice rising as he informed her, 'I'd be bored stiff in five minutes flat. I'd prefer to fight with my wife than make love to any other woman on the planet.' And after the fighting, he thought, a smile tugging at the corners of his mouth, they would make love.

Carla stared at him, shook her head. 'You don't love her…you can't *love* her.'

'My wife would tell you straight away, Carla, that telling me not to do something only encourages me to go right out and do it. But enough. I have no idea what sick fantasies you have been nursing, and frankly I don't want to know, my stomach is not that strong—'

This deliberate cruelty drew a gasp of shock from the brunette.

'My only priority is getting my pregnant wife back safe and sound.'

'How do you even know the baby is yours?' Of course, the moment the spiteful words left her lips Carla knew that she had gone too far. Shaking her head, she began to back away as Gianfranco, his dark eyes like ice chips, was advancing on her with all the menace of a sleek, ruthless tiger.

'What have you done to her?'

She continued back, holding her hands in front of her as if to ward him off. 'I haven't done anything,' she babbled. 'Nothing. When I arrived she was already about to set off.'

Gianfranco stopped. 'Set off where?'

'She said that you and Alberto had gone camping in the mountains somewhere. That you wouldn't know about the storm and Alberto had told her there was no phone reception there,' she said.

'Camping, but we cancelled that trip weeks ago.' The moment he had realised that the proposed father-son trip—a yearly ritual of male bonding—to the remote mountain cabin was within weeks of the birth.

His fear of the baby coming early had made him decide to work from home after the weekend, but Dervla didn't know that because he hadn't told her.

Carla's expression settled into pouting petulance as she retorted, 'Well, she seemed to think you were there.' From the way she was looking at him he suspected that being the next Mrs Bruni had lost a lot of its attraction. 'And she was quite rude to me.'

'Rude to you when you didn't try and stop her?' Even as he made the accusation Gianfranco knew that if anything happened to Dervla and his unborn child it wouldn't be Carla's fault, it would be his.

It would be his because he had cornered the market in self-delusion. It would be his because he had barely talked to his wife for weeks, because he knew that if he did he might hear the words, 'I love you' coming out of his mouth!

He pushed aside the self-condemnatory reflections. Time enough for those later; now he had to get to Dervla before the storm struck. She didn't know the exact location of the cabin, but she did, he realised, know the road they took to it.

She knew because they had been driving past soon after they were first married. He had been annoyed because they were late for a dinner engagement because of Dervla's infuriatingly relaxed attitude to time-keeping. He couldn't decide if she really lacked a sense of urgency or she did it to aggravate him.

'Maybe you should take a short cut.'

'What short cut?' he asked without removing his eyes from the road ahead.

'That one,' she explained, indicating the unmade mountain track they were driving past.

'That road is a short cut nowhere. The only place it leads is the cabin we use for camping trips, and it's prone to landslides in wet weather. Nobody but an *imbecile* would attempt it without a four-wheel drive.'

'Well, that hardly excludes you, does it? And if you're in a hurry to reach your grave that would prove the perfect short cut.'

'Are you suggesting I'm not a good driver? For your information I am considered…' Their eyes meshed briefly, and the amused gleam in hers caused him to close his mouth over any further defence of his motor skills.

'Call a man a bad driver—would I dare? No, call me a nervous passenger with an unreasonable desire to get to my destination in one piece.'

He had not responded to the jibe but he had slowed down.

Dervla was heading for that road; the thought made his blood congeal in his veins with icy horror.

'*Madre di Dio*, the little idiot!' he whispered. He flashed Carla a look that made the woman grow pale and said grimly, 'Don't be here when I get back.' And hoped she would have the sense to believe him when he added, 'Because I really won't be responsible for my actions if a hair on Dervla's head is hurt.'

Then he hit the floor running.

Dervla had gone about halfway up the rough track before it became obvious her car wouldn't be going any farther. She unfastened her seat belt and recalled Gianfranco's comments concerning this road, four-wheel drives and imbeciles.

It might have been more useful if she had recalled them a mile back, but a mile back she'd been running on adrenaline, panic and the misplaced notion that Gianfranco, just about the most resourceful and self-sufficient man on the planet, needed her help to keep safe.

She sat, elbows braced on the dashboard, her nose pressed close to the windscreen, staring through the rain that hammered against the glass at the large boulder that had presumably come from the cliff above.

Well, he was wrong on one count: even a four-wheel drive couldn't have got past that. There was barely enough room for a bicycle to pass, or a person foolhardy enough to complete their journey on foot.

On the imbecile part she was on shakier ground.

It wasn't her plan that was bad, just her timing. If she had managed to reach them before the rain started this would have been nothing more than a pleasant stroll.

But the rain had started and it showed no sign of stopping any time soon. She considered her options—they were limited.

She could wait in the car or she could find the cabin. Well, how far could it be?

She switched off the engine and told herself sternly not to be a wimp. A little bit of drizzle never hurt anyone.

But, said the voice in her head, there was always a first time. And *little* was possibly not the most accurate description, nor had it been drizzle for a good fifteen minutes. The sound of the torrential deluge battering down was deafening without the background engine noise.

At some point this must have seemed like a good idea, but Dervla was no longer sure when or why. Still, like the swimmer who was already halfway across the river, it was easier to go on than turn back.

Or she could stay put? Stay dry and safe until another massive boulder crashed down the mountain and landed on her little car.

The possibility had her scrambling out of the car as fast as her increased girth and altered centre of gravity would allow.

She was drenched to the skin literally before she even closed the car door…a bit of a struggle as the squally wind was a lot stronger than she had anticipated. As she stumbled upwards, head bent, teeth gritted, she didn't allow herself to think beyond the next step until about ten exhausting minutes later there was no next step.

There was no road; it just stopped. The ground rose steeply to her right, there was a dizzying drop to her left and up ahead there was terrain similar to that she had already covered—minus any sign of a track or even footpath.

Struggling to catch her breath, she wiped the moisture from her face and squinted ahead. A distant rumble of thunder made her jump.

'*Great!* Just what I need!' she yelled at the sky, tilting her head to glare at the leaden greyness overhead as she struggled to hold back the tears and the fear.

Dervla couldn't afford to acknowledge the fear she could feel lodged like a lump of ice behind her breastbone. If she did she knew she would succumb to the gibbering panic that was so close she could smell it.

'You're about as much use as a neurotic Saint Bernard with no sense of direction, Dervla.' While she delivered this scathing indictment on her abilities as a rescue party her thoughts raced.

She closed her eyes and shook her head, wondering at the primal instincts that had kicked in when she had thought Gianfranco and Alberto were in danger.

What did I think I was going to do? It wasn't as if Gianfranco was exactly helpless, he was resourceful enough to cope with just about anything anyone threw at him.

They were probably tucked up in the cabin in front of a roaring log fire, oblivious to or, more likely knowing the way a Bruni male's mind worked, *stimulated by* the raging elements outside.

Oh, how I wish I were with them. She took a deep breath and lifted her chin as she said out loud, 'Well, you're not going to find them feeling sorry for yourself, Dervla.'

The baby inside, as if hearing her bracing words, aimed an extra strong kick and she winced. Will you inherit the same fearless nature? she wondered, pressing her hand to her belly.

Her expression hardened into a mask of bleak self-condemnation. Will you get the opportunity?

What sort of mother was she, risking her baby's life this way? Her face set in lines of determination.

'I got us into this, baby, so it is up to me to get us out.'

Now where, she asked herself, is that cabin?

CHAPTER FIFTEEN

GIANFRANCO found the car. It was hard not to. The hatchback Dervla had chosen in preference to the sleek sports car he had presented her with was slewed across the track.

He searched the interior methodically. Her bag and a thin jacket were in the back seat, the keys were still in the ignition, but there were no obvious signs to indicate she had been injured. He allowed the air to leave his lungs, not aware until that moment that he had been holding his breath.

He pulled the keys from the ignition. These weren't the keys he had originally presented her with, or the car that he had intended for his new wife to drive. A rueful smile momentarily lightened the grim bleakness of his expression.

He had been so damn pleased with himself. There was a waiting list a mile long for the gleaming new model—a waiting list he had managed to skip to the top of in order to give his wife the best.

And had she been impressed? No, not Dervla—she had walked around the vehicle, clearly searching for something nice to say about it.

'It's very nice. A lovely colour.'

'You don't like it.' He was surprised at how piqued he felt that the gift had not produced the squeals of delight he had anticipated.

'It's beautiful,' she hastened to assure him.

'*But…?*' He ought to have known better. Since when did Dervla react like other women and since when was she impressed by status symbols?

'Just not really *me*…and think how bad I'd feel if I scraped it.' She shuddered at the thought. 'A little second-hand runabout would suit me fine.'

'My wife will not drive around in "a second-hand runabout".'

But of course she had, because he had given in as usual, and just look at the result. Well, in future he wouldn't be so easily swayed, he decided grimly. And Dervla wouldn't be driving around in anything. He had no intention of letting her out of his sight for the foreseeable future!

The storm was at its peak as he set off at a trot up the half-blocked track. Thinking about Dervla alone out there in this just tore him to pieces inside. What the hell was that woman trying to do to him? When he found her he'd…*if* he found her…

Jaw set, the sinews standing out like wire in his neck, he banished from his mind the nightmare mental image of a body lying twisted and broken at the bottom of a ravine. This was not a moment to permit his rampant imagination off the mental leash.

Negative thinking had never been his style and he wasn't about to change now. He knew if he opened the door on that raw animal fear that lay coiled in his belly it would paralyse him. He *would* find her alive and, well…then he would throttle her for doing this to him.

It was ten minutes later that he did find she was alive and well. There was no time to throttle her. She was walking along a dried-up river bed. He came up behind her and spoke her name, raising his voice to make himself heard against the wind.

She hadn't heard his approach and began to struggle, arms and legs flailing wildly before she recognised him.

When she did the fight went out of her body and she began to weep and say his name over and over. Gianfranco could feel the tremors running through her body like a fever.

He held her close as she pushed her head into his shoulder and wound her arms around his neck so tightly he had to loosen them in order to breathe.

He closed his eyes and breathed in the scent of her hair. He was dizzy with relief, exultant. He had seen in these last nightmare minutes life without Dervla and he knew in the depths of his soul that he held the one person that gave his life any sort of meaning.

He wanted to tell her what she meant to him. The words were there on his tongue as he tilted her pale tear-stained little face up to him.

The memory of the primal fear he had experienced flooded through him as he thought, *I nearly lost you!* Before he heard himself yell.

'I have had not a moment's peace since we met. Do you try and do imbecilic things or can you not stop yourself?'

He saw the hurt surface in her glazed eyes, then the anger that followed in its wake.

'I was trying to save you.' Dervla tensed, waiting for the sarcastic retort her protest invited, but it didn't come. 'I didn't know you didn't need saving. You said that you and Alberto were going to the cabin,' she added defensively. 'I thought you were picking him up straight from school and I knew there was no signal and I thought if I hurried I could get to you before the storm and warn you—'

'You jumped in your car and decided to save us.' How many women would have the guts to do that? 'You are eight months pregnant!'

She coloured with embarrassment; in retrospect it was pretty hard to defend her actions. '*Warn* you about the storm.'

'You are always pointing out how many staff we have. I seem to recall you wondering if I could actually tie my shoelaces without assistance. Did it not occur to you to delegate the task to one of them, or even contact the emergency services?'

The dots of colour on her pale cheeks darkened. 'I panicked,' she admitted miserably. She wiped a hand across her face to blot the excess moisture and blinked up at him, struggling to hold back the tears. 'Alberto is all right?'

'Alberto is fine. There was no trip. I cancelled it weeks ago.'

Dervla knew how sacrosanct the time he put aside to spend with his son was. It must have been something particularly important to make him cancel the trip. And he was missing the important something because of her.

She opened her mouth to apologise and closed it. When emotions were running this high it was pretty hard to keep a guard on your tongue and she was afraid what indiscretions might slip out once she started talking.

He watched as she bit her trembling lip, wanting very much to kiss her, but aware they had already lingered too long.

He knew how dangerous these dry beds could be after the rain in the hills. Flash-floods were commonplace even when there was no rainfall this low down. Gianfranco had seen livestock that had strayed into them washed away in the torrent. It was not uncommon for people ignorant of the dangers to suffer the same fate.

'What are you…?' Dervla's voice rose in a shrill cry of protest as he unceremoniously picked her up.

'Have you ever seen a flash-flood?' he asked, setting her down a moment later in the safety of a spot protected from the wind by a large boulder, before turning her around to face him. Without waiting for her response he ground out grimly, 'Well, I have.'

Dervla's eyes flickered to the dry river bed. 'Aren't you being a bit dramatic?' She gave a nervous laugh that visibly annoyed him and pointed out, 'It isn't even raining that much now.' Despite her bravado the thought of being caught in a raging torrent made her already weak knees tremble.

'Dramatic!' Gianfranco thundered, slamming his fist against the boulder, appearing oblivious to the pain caused by his grazed knuckles. Closing his eyes, he inhaled deeply and threw back his head, raising his face to the sky.

Dervla felt a stab of awe as she looked at him. He made a sybaritic image, sable hair slicked wetly to his skull, the water sliding down his bronzed face glistening. He looked as perfect as a classical statue, but so much more alive. The air around him seemed to crackle with the male vitality he exuded. There was something in Gianfranco, she realised, that was as raw and elemental as the storm itself.

He looked beautiful, and she…? Dervla's mouth twisted into an ironic grimace as her glance slid downwards; she didn't need a mirror to know that she looked like an extra in a horror film.

'You always have to have the last word, don't you?'

Dervla's eyes lifted, then fell from the dark, accusing fury in his. She could understand his anger; so far she hadn't even said thank you. And he was no doubt reflecting on all the things he'd prefer to be doing in preference to chasing his slightly mad, very pregnant wife over a mountain in a storm.

'How did you know where I'd be?'

'Carla was at the house,' he said shortly.

'Was she very worried?'

He gave an odd laugh. 'Not so that you'd notice. Your face…' He swore, his jaw clenching as he noticed for the first time the red scratch that ran down one smooth cheek. He tilted her face a little one way to get a better view, then, satisfied the wound was superficial, let his fingers fall away. 'How did you do it?' he asked thickly.

'What?' she asked, wishing he had not released her. It was ridiculous, but even his lightest touch lowered her anxiety levels. She lifted her hand to her face and felt the scratch. 'I didn't feel it.'

His eyes, dark and burning like the coals deep in a furnace, moved restlessly across her face as he planted his hands heavily on her shoulders.

'Are you hurt anywhere else?' His voice was gentle, but there was a rasp, a catch almost, in his deep vibrant voice as his hands skimmed down her body.

His touch was clinical, her reaction was not, which was, in the circumstances, Dervla told herself, faintly ludicrous. You have all the sexual allure of a baby elephant, she told herself. He had not shared her bed for many weeks.

Not since he learned of her pregnancy.

'No, I'm fine.'

'You are not fine. You are shaking like a leaf still,' he discovered.

Dervla shrugged as he took off his jacket and placed it around her shoulders. What was she meant to say—I'm shaking because you're touching me?

'You'll get cold,' she protested as he pulled the lapels of the jacket together under her chin.

His long brown fingers touched the side of her face as their eyes meshed. 'I will survive.'

'You must think I'm a total idiot.'

There was a pause, it stretched and Dervla struggled and failed to disentangle her eyes from his.

There was strain etched into his finely chiselled features when he finally responded. 'No, I think *I* am a total idiot.'

Once, not long ago, he would have stigmatised any man who imagined himself in love an idiot, but now Gianfranco recognised that falling in love might be the most sensible thing he had done in his entire life. It was his own stubborn refusal to recognise the fact that filled Gianfranco with contempt.

The response when it came felt like a slap in the face to Dervla. He had never come out and said it before—that he regretted marrying her.

'We can't stay here.' He scanned the horizon. 'We need some shelter.'

'You can't carry me!' she protested.

His attitude was not one of compromise as he scooped her up and suggested that she hold on, adding firmly, 'You can't walk in your condition.'

'But I'm heavy.'

'I work out.'

'I'd noticed.' Me and every other female with a pulse! 'And I had assumed you hadn't run to flab since the last time I saw you without your shirt.' Dervla closed her eyes. Even she could hear the wistful note in her voice.

It only took him five minutes to locate the cabin. Dervla realised she had never at any point been very far from it.

Inside the cabin was basic: one room with a stone grate one end, and bunks the other. The only other furniture was a wooden table and two chairs.

Gianfranco took one of the chairs, set it in front of the stone grate and indicated with an inclination of his head that she should sit in it.

'Not much in the way of creature comforts, but at least it's dry in here.'

Dervla waited for pain in her back to pass, glancing out of the window before she lowered herself cautiously into the chair. She still wouldn't allow herself to think what the back pain might mean. When her baby came it was going to be born in a clean, safe hospital.

'Do you think the storm will last long?'

'Who knows?'

Unable to share his lack of concern, she watched, her jaw clenched, as Gianfranco opened a wooden chest set a little to one side of the fire and took out a box of matches and a bundle of dry kindling.

'But won't it be dark soon?'

Having a baby was the most natural thing in the world... home births were becoming increasingly popular, though admittedly usually in homes with phones and running water. Not that the question even arose; she had another month to go. Goodness, if a person imagined she was in labour every time she had a little twinge, she for one would have spent the last month pointlessly dashing to hospital.

Gianfranco slung her a quizzical look over his shoulder before he knelt down in front of the fire. 'You are afraid of the dark… I didn't think you were afraid of anything.'

Dervla, missing the admiration in his observation, took it to be a taunt, a suggestion she didn't possess any of the feminine frailities he no doubt found appealing, and was on her feet in one angry rush. 'Not afraid!' she repeated, her voice shaking. 'I'm afraid of everything!'

At that moment having her baby in a hut on top of a mountain with no running water or medical assistance rated pretty high on her list of fears. As quickly as it came the anger and the burst of energy that accompanied it left her. Lifting a hand to her head in a weary gesture, she sank back into the chair very aware of Gianfranco staring at her.

'You're not afraid of me.' For a man who struggled to find people with enough guts to look him in the eye and say, 'No, you're wrong,' this was rare. A smile quivered on his lips as he accused, 'You've not stopped trying to put me in my place since we met.'

Aware that she had overreacted dramatically, Dervla took refuge from his far too perceptive stare behind the shield of her lashes. 'Without any conspicuous success,' she retorted gruffly.

'That rather depends on where you think my place is.' If anyone had suggested to him a year ago that he would ever contemplate telling a woman that his place was in her heart he would have either laughed or referred them to a psychiatrist. And now here he was, a man never at a loss for words, struggling to find the right syllables.

'Don't worry, there's a torch somewhere.'

'A torch!' she echoed bitterly. 'Why didn't you say so? Great, a torch—all of our problems are solved.'

Her main problem right now, Dervla reflected, was keeping her mouth closed on the smart little one-liners. She was terrified but Gianfranco would assume she was just plain nasty and ungrateful.

'Look,' she said quietly. 'I'm sorry if I put you to a lot of trouble.'

He turned his head slowly. Dervla returned his stare warily, unable to interpret his expression, or the almost incandescent glow in his burning eyes. His body language was less baffling. The branch he had been about to feed onto the fire snapped between his long fingers.

'Put me to trouble…?' he echoed in the strangest voice she had ever heard.

She nodded and decided the apology was long overdue even if he did think it was inadequate. 'I know I've been a nuisance and I know sorry is not much of a recompense for messing up your day and stranding you here, but I am…sorry, that is.'

He rubbed the groove between his brows and muttered, 'She says this to me…*Madre di Dio*!' Shaking his head, he closed his eyes and ran a hand across the dark stubble on his lower face.

The silence stretched, broken by the rain against the window-pane and the crackle of the logs in the grate.

'I really am sorry, Gianfranco.'

At the sound of her unhappy voice, Gianfranco's heavy lids lifted. His compelling dark stare burned into her as he said thickly, 'I have been to hell today thinking you were lying hurt and needing me, or worse.' He passed a hand across his eyes as though to extinguish the nightmare images that his imagination had tortured him with.

'I would gladly have given my soul if it meant having you back safe.' He reached out and clamped a hand that had a perceptive tremor to her belly. 'You, and our child,' he said thickly.

Dervla stared like someone in a dream at his brown fingers. She could feel the blood as it thundered in her ears. In her chest her heart was pounding frantically against her ribcage.

She shook her head, unable to give herself permission to believe the things he was telling her.

He didn't mean it literally, she told herself as she fitted her small hand over his. Only Gianfranco didn't say things for dramatic effect—he said things when he meant them.

So why was he saying these things?

He was too young to be suffering a mid-life crisis. Maybe living with me has tipped him over the edge?

Before you go saying or doing something silly, just remember, she told herself, he wanted a mistress, he got a wife and a baby, and neither item had ever been on his wish list.

Her eyes fell to the brown fingers under her own; his big hand felt warm through the thin, wet material of her dress. Her throat closed over heavy and thick with emotion that brought the sting of hot, unshed tears to her eyes.

If they could stay like this for ever she would never feel afraid again, only she *was* afraid, Dervla realised. Afraid if she moved this perfect moment would be gone and all she'd have left would be a memory.

'You don't want a baby,' she felt impelled to remind him. 'And I understand,' she hurried to assure him. 'You feel you're being disloyal to Alberto's mum.'

Surprise flashed in his eyes. 'The feelings I had for Sara bear no resemblance to what I feel for you,' he retorted with a frown.

Dervla arranged her features into a smile while inside she was crying her heart out. 'I realise that,' she told him quietly. 'I know she was the great love of your life and I'd never try and compete.' A dead saint was pretty hard to compete with.

Gianfranco gave an incredulous laugh. 'The way your mind works is a constant source of amazement to me, *cara*.' He shook his head. 'Did you work out that all by yourself?

Or did you,' he speculated, 'have a little help, from cousin Carla perhaps…?'

Dervla felt obliged to defend the older woman. 'Carla wasn't telling me anything that isn't common knowledge. It's not like it's a secret. I understand that it's too painful for you to talk about.'

'You understand nothing,' he bit back.

A surge of emotion washed over her at his emphatic response. 'Because I suppose I'm not capable of comprehending that sort of grand passion? You're not the only one who has feelings, you know,' she cried, pressing a hand to her heaving bosom as a dry sob escaped her aching throat.

'The reason I don't talk about Sara or our marriage is because it's painful—painful because nobody likes to dredge up their mistakes and there is Alberto to consider—'

'Mistake?' she echoed, thinking she must have misheard.

'Not Alberto,' Gianfranco hastened to assure her. 'Though if Sara had had her way there would have been no Alberto.'

'She didn't want a baby?' Dervla tried not to sound shocked, but such a thing seemed inexplicable to her. What could be more fulfilling than having the child of the man you loved?

'I persuaded her not to have the abortion and marry me instead.' He turned his head, making it impossible for Dervla to see his face when he added bleakly, 'And I suppose you could say that makes me directly responsible for her death.'

'What are you talking about, Gianfranco?' She touched his shoulder and could immediately feel the tension in his bunched muscles.

'Sara developed diabetes during pregnancy. The doctors said that it would go away once the baby was born.'

'And it didn't?' Dervla probed gently.

He shook his head. 'She needed injections twice a day and she hated them. At first they struggled to stabilise her, but she had been fine for months when…she had a hypoglycaemic attack when she was shopping, but people thought she was drunk. The symptoms are not that dissimilar. By the time someone realised she was ill it was too late. She was dead before she reached the hospital.'

As she listened to the tragic story, made all the more poignant because of the flat monotone voice she knew concealed his deep feelings, Dervla's eyes filled. 'That is really terrible, but not your fault.'

He rose from his position at her feet and moved to take a seat beside her on the wooden bench.

'I was nineteen and starting up my first company when I met Sara. I was full of romantic ideals and raging hormones—a dangerous combination,' he observed wryly. 'I was pretty intense in those days and inclined to take myself rather seriously.

'I wrote poetry.' He made the admission as though he were confessing to some awful vice.

'You wrote poetry? Was it good poetry?'

'Actually it was nauseatingly bad. I must have been incredibly boring, but she was a nice girl, a good-looking girl and more interested in sex than the meaning of life, which made her a lot more intelligent than me,' he said matter-of-factly.

'I honestly think that Sara found me a little odd, and I know she wouldn't have married me if I hadn't already made my first million. I'm not saying she was predatory or avaricious or anything of that sort, just, well…tempted by the lifestyle.'

'You loved her,' Dervla protested weakly.

His lips curled into a sneer. *'Loved!'* he ejaculated contemptuously. 'Maybe there are nineteen-year-olds who know the meaning of the word, but I was not one of them. I didn't know the meaning of the word until very recently—'

Dervla's wide green eyes flew to his face. She felt numb with disbelief. 'You don't love me, Gianfranco…?'

'How could I not?' he asked thickly. 'Even when I could not accept my feelings for what they were I loved you. I rationalised my actions, my feelings, but since the moment I met you I have been trying to bind you to me.'

He caught hold of her hands and held on as though he would never let her go. 'I hope one day you will be able to forgive me…I cannot forgive myself, but it was my fear speaking. Sara died because she carried my child. If I lost you…' He turned to her and the terrible bleakness in his eyes struck like a spear to her heart.

'You're not going to lose me, Gianfranco,' she promised huskily.

'If I did…' He closed his eyes and shuddered. 'From the moment I laid eyes on you I started feeling things I didn't want to, things I was terrified to let myself feel. I was too much of a coward to admit even to myself that what I felt for you was love. You were, you are, the soul mate I decided did not exist.'

Tears slid silently down her cheeks as she took his face between her hands and pressed her lips to his. When they broke apart they were both breathing hard.

'You moved out of our bed,' she accused, half laughing, half crying. Her mind was still struggling to cope with all the shocks.

'I thought,' he confessed, 'that was what you wanted. I was trying to be sensitive.' He shook his head and grimaced. 'It was hell.'

This admission drew a laugh from her. 'Don't do sensitive. It really doesn't suit you. You're the arrogant unable-to-express-his-feelings type, although I might have to rethink the expression-of-feelings area after today.' Her smile deepened as her glowing eyes rested on his lean, dark, beloved face. 'My type actually. You're just—' She broke off, wincing.

'What's wrong?'

'Nothing's wrong, exactly.' I hope.

'Then…'

She patted his hand. 'Now, don't panic, but I think—well, actually I'm pretty sure the baby is coming.'

He patted her head and said indulgently, 'No, the baby isn't due for another four weeks.'

'Tell him that,' she suggested, patting her belly just as another contraction hit.

Gianfranco's mind went a total blank as he watched her pant her way through the wave.

When it was over she straightened up, her anxious eyes immediately going to his face. 'Are you all right?'

She was asking him that?

Gianfranco felt a wave of shame as he kicked free of the paralysing fear. His brain cleared and he dropped to his knees in front of her and took her small hands within his.

'All right? I'm going to be a father. I'm terrified.' He accompanied his words with a grin she appeared to find reassuring.

'Me too, actually.'

'How hard can it be? People do it every day.'

'Not people,' she retorted, pretending indignation. 'Women. Like to swap places?'

Actually, given the opportunity to take on her burden, take her pain on himself, Gianfranco would not have hesitated, but, that not being an option, he had to work with what they had. A glance around the cabin revealed that was precious little.

'I suppose you couldn't cope with me carrying you down to the car?'

She shook her head.

'Fine. You're a nurse.'

'A nurse, not a midwife. I've never delivered a baby.'

'Don't worry, we'll be fine. I'm not without experience.' His internet research had been limited to abnormal births, so he sincerely hoped than none of that information would come in useful.

'You've delivered a baby?'

'A foal, but the basic concept,' he contended, 'is much the same.'

Dervla's laughter was slightly strained, but she did seem a

little more relaxed. 'I think maybe I should walk. It helps get things moving.'

Gianfranco wasn't so sure he wanted things to get moving, but he went along with the suggestion, helping her to get to her feet and providing an arm for her to lean on as she walked slowly up and down the room, stopping and breathing through it when a contraction hit her.

He was actually starting to think this wasn't so bad when she didn't so much breathe as scream— quite loudly, actually, and in his ear.

Madre di Dio!

'What, *cara*, is after the walking part?' He sincerely hoped whatever it was didn't involve too much screaming, but he suspected it did. Conscious that it was his job to be supportive— well, compared to what she was doing it wasn't a big task—he smiled encouragingly.

'I might have missed that class, but I think it might be a good time.' Smothering her growing panic, she smiled. The last thing she wanted to do was traumatise him more.

Gianfranco dragged the mattresses from the bunks and put them on the floor. After settling her on them, he looked around for some sort of container. In all the old films he had seen boiled water was the factor common to all.

'Look, let me tell you some stuff before…well, I might not feel much like giving instructions come the time.'

'Good idea.'

He listened and understood about half and suspected he'd have forgotten most of the stuff he did register when the moment came.

'Right, you just relax and conserve your energy.'

The advice seemed a little misplaced when it became obvious as the contractions slid seamlessly into one another that rest was not an option. To watch her suffer and be totally unable to do anything about it was just about the most frustrating thing that had ever happened to Gianfranco.

'It can't be long now,' he soothed as she flopped, her face beaded with the sweat that soaked her red hair. He clenched the hand she had squeezed to return the circulation to his white, bloodless fingers.

'Not long now,' she said abruptly. 'I have to push.'

'Are you meant to?'

'I have to!' she told him fiercely.

This stage was relatively quick. It barely seemed any time at all before he was crying out in wonder as the baby's head crowned and then moments later their daughter slipped, warm, wet and screaming her lungs out, into his waiting hands.

'Is she all right?' Dervla cried, trying to lever herself upright.

'She is totally perfect,' he breathed, staring in wonder at the screaming bundle. He kissed Dervla, brushed the hair back from her damp brow and said with total sincerity, 'You were incredible…brilliant,' before he placed the baby on her breast.

The sight of her face as she held their baby for the first time—the sheer wonder in her face, the maternal love shining in her eyes—it would stay with him for ever.

He barely had time to turn his thoughts to the next problem of how they were going to get down from here when the door opened.

The paramedic walked in, grinned when he took in the scene and said, 'Nothing much left for me to do.'

The man explained the situation in rapid Italian that Dervla, in her bemused condition, couldn't follow, but when he left them for a moment Gianfranco translated.

'Apparently Alberto called in the cavalry. There's a helicopter waiting to airlift you and this little one to hospital.'

Watching his face as he kissed the fiery nimbus of curls that topped their daughter's head tenderly made Dervla's eyes fill with emotional tears.

She caught his hand. 'I'm not going anywhere without you.'

Gianfranco smiled into her eyes. 'You must, *cara mia*, but I promise you we will not be separated for long. We will never be separated. Not until you get so tired of my face you kick me out.'

'I could never get tired of your face,' she promised, gazing up at him, her eyes blazing with the love that spilled out of her. 'I love you, Gianfranco, and thank you for giving me my miracle. You were incredible. I couldn't have done it without you here. I wouldn't have wanted to.'

'Our miracle,' he corrected firmly. 'There is only one thing I want to get clear right now. If we are ever lucky enough to have any more miracles…you are staying within a one-mile radius of a hospital for the last two months minimum.'

'What, no home birth?' she teased.

'I am learning with you it is not a good thing to say never— you consider it a challenge. So I will simply say I am content with our family as it is now. The future—well, that will take care of itself and I will take care of you and our family.'

Dervla snuggled their baby to her breast. She could see no flaw whatever in his plan, and any future that had Gianfranco in it was, she was sure, going to be better than good!

EPILOGUE

GIANFRANCO dragged a hand through his dark hair. 'I don't believe this!'

The chauffeur's glance slid to his employer and he gave an apologetic grimace. 'Apparently a lorry overturned on the junction…'

Gianfranco's frustration exploded. 'It didn't occur to you to check before we left? There's no way around!'

'Gianfranco, it's no use yelling. It's not his fault. I'm sorry, Eduardo, take no notice of him.'

With a small smile the chauffeur inclined his head carefully, not looking in the direction of his explosive employer.

Once the door closed Gianfranco turned to his wife with an outraged expression. 'Are you not concerned?' he demanded.

She smiled serenely back at him. 'Why should I be?' she asked, patting her stomach. 'I have a perfectly capable midwife in the car with me. Daddy was good enough for you, wasn't he, darling?' she said to the little girl.

Valeria was eighteen months old. She had her mother's fiery hair, her father's eyes and a smile that was all her own. Her half-brother was her willing slave and her father was wrapped around her chubby little finger.

'This baby will be born in a hospital with doctors and clean linen.'

'If he's anything like his father he will be born exactly where he likes.' An early scan had revealed pretty conclusively that the new arrival was male.

'I cannot believe lightning is striking in the same place twice.'

'Hardly the same place, Gianfranco,' his wife protested, repressing a smile at his agitation. 'This is hardly a mountain-top in Tuscany.'

'Now it's the outside lane of a motorway, which is hardly an improvement. Oh, *cara*, I'm so sorry. I wanted it to be perfect for you this time after what you endured. And this happens!' he observed with disgust.

Dervla gazed lovingly into the face of her handsome husband. 'Oh, Gianfranco, last time was perfect for me. I always knew nothing was going to top that, and I do wish you'd stop stressing. I could have stayed home for hours yet. I'm still in the very early stages. I might just as well sit here as in a hospital ward.'

Gianfranco seemed slightly soothed by her calm observations. 'I suppose you're right. But how can you say last time was perfect? It was the most terrifying couple of hours of my life. Your life and Val's was in my hands.'

'There are no hands I would prefer to be in,' she said, taking one strong brown hand and pressing it lovingly to her cheek. 'The point is it was scary, it was frankly terrifying, but it was also the most marvellous moments of my life. You told me you loved me and you brought our miracle baby into the world. How can anything be better than that?' she asked simply. 'And I know this baby will be safe. I feel it.' She took his hand and pressed it to her belly.

'Did you feel that?' he exclaimed.

Dervla laughed. 'It's kind of hard not to, and one of the reasons I am looking forward to meeting this centre forward in person.'

'And then I think our family is complete…three children is enough for any man. I don't want to be greedy,' he observed, then spoiled the rather pious observation by saying with a sigh, 'As sexy as you look when you're pregnant, I'm looking forward to having you to myself again.'

'The traffic's moving.'

Gianfranco let out a cheer, which Valeria enthusiastically joined in, clapping her fat little hands. 'Well, thank God for that!'

'Actually, Gianfranco, I think it might be an idea to ask Eduardo to turn around.'

His face fell comically. 'Another false alarm?'

She nodded. 'Sorry.'

'You know,' he observed gloomily, 'I have a sneaky feeling this baby is going to come when we least expect it. He's trying to lull us into a false sense of security,' he mused darkly.

'Really, Gianfranco, you can be quite silly sometimes,' Dervla observed indulgently.

Roman Antonio was born, weighing eight pounds two, at two a.m. the next morning, after they decided he was another false alarm. He dropped into his father's hands bawling his head off.

* * * * *

THOROUGHBRED LEGACY
*The stakes are high when it comes to love,
horse racing, family secrets
and broken promises.*

*A new exciting Harlequin continuity series coming soon!
Led by* New York Times *bestselling author Elizabeth Bevarly*
FLIRTING WITH TROUBLE

Here's a preview

THE DOOR CLOSED behind them, throwing them into darkness and leaving them utterly alone. And the next thing Daniel knew, he heard himself saying, "Marnie, I'm sorry about the way things turned out in Del Mar."

She said nothing at first, only strode across the room and stared out the window beside him. Although he couldn't see her well in the darkness—he still hadn't switched on a light…but then, neither had she—he imagined her expression was a little preoccupied, a little anxious, a little confused.

Finally, very softly, she said, "Are you?"

He nodded, then, worried she wouldn't be able to see the gesture, added, "Yeah. I am. I should have said goodbye to you."

"Yes, you should have."

Actually, he thought, there were a lot of things he should have done in Del Mar. He'd had *a lot* riding on the Pacific Classic, and even more on his entry, Little Joe, but after meeting Marnie, the Pacific Classic had been the last thing on Daniel's mind. His loss at Del Mar had pretty much ended his career before it had even begun, and he'd had to start all over again, rebuilding from nothing.

He simply had not then and did not now have room in his life for a woman as potent as Marnie Roberts. He was a horseman first and foremost. From the time he was a school-boy, he'd known what he wanted to do with his life—be the best possible trainer he could be.

He had to make sure Marnie understood—and he understood, too—why things had ended the way they had eight years ago. He just wished he could find the words to do that. Hell, he wished he could find the *thoughts* to do that.

"You made me forget things, Marnie, things that I really needed to remember. And that scared the hell out of me. Little Joe should have won the Classic. He was by far the best horse entered in that race. But I didn't give him the attention he needed and deserved that week, because all I could think about was you. Hell, when I woke up that morning all I wanted to do was lie there and look at you, and then wake you up and make love to you again. If I hadn't left when I did—the way I did—I might still be lying there in that bed with you, thinking about nothing else."

"And would that be so terrible?" she asked.

"Of course not," he told her. "But that wasn't why I was in Del Mar," he repeated. "I was in Del Mar to win a race. That was my job. And my work was the most important thing to me."

She said nothing for a moment, only studied his face in the darkness as if looking for the answer to a very important question. Finally she asked, "And what's the most important thing to you now, Daniel?"

Wasn't the answer to that obvious? "My work," he answered automatically.

She nodded slowly. "Of course," she said softly. "That is, after all, what you do best."

Her comment, too, puzzled him. She made it sound as if being good at what he did was a bad thing.

She bit her lip thoughtfully, her eyes fixed on his, glimmering in the scant moonlight that was filtering through the window. And damned if Daniel didn't find himself wanting to pull her into his arms and kiss her. But as much as it might have felt as if no time had passed since Del Mar, there were eight years between now and then. And eight years was a long time in the best of circumstances. For Daniel and Marnie, it was virtually a lifetime.

So Daniel turned and started for the door, then halted. He couldn't just walk away and leave things as they were, unsettled. He'd done that eight years ago and regretted it.

"It *was* good to see you again, Marnie," he said softly. And since he was being honest, he added, "I hope we see each other again."

She didn't say anything in response, only stood silhouetted against the window with her arms wrapped around her in a way that made him wonder whether she was doing it because she was cold, or if she just needed something—someone—to hold on to. In either case, Daniel understood. There was an emptiness clinging to him that he suspected would be there for a long time.

* * * * *

THOROUGHBRED LEGACY
coming soon wherever books are sold!

Don't miss the brilliant
new novel from

Natalie Rivers

featuring a dark, dangerous
and decadent Italian!

THE SALVATORE
MARRIAGE DEAL

Available June 2008
Book #2735

*Look out for more books
from Natalie Rivers coming soon,
only in Harlequin Presents!*

HARLEQUIN *Presents*

What do you look for in a guy?
Charisma. Sex appeal. Confidence.
A body to die for. Well, look no further
this series has men with all this and more!
And now that they've met the women in these novels,
there is one thing on everyone's mind....

NIGHTS *of* PASSION

One night is never enough!

**The guys know what they want
and how they're going to get it!**

Don't miss:

HIS MISTRESS
BY ARRANGEMENT

by

Natalie Anderson

Available June 2008.

*Look out for more Nights of Passion,
coming soon in Harlequin Presents!*

www.eHarlequin.com

HP12737

Harlequin Presents brings you
a brand-new duet by star author

Sharon Kendrick

THE GREEK BILLIONAIRES' BRIDES

Power, pride and passion—discover how only
the love and passion of two women can reunite
these wealthy, successful brothers,
divided by a bitter rivalry.

Available June 2008:

THE GREEK TYCOON'S
BABY BARGAIN

Available July 2008:

THE GREEK TYCOON'S
CONVENIENT WIFE

I ♥

HARLEQUIN® *Presents*

BROUGHT TO YOU BY FANS OF
HARLEQUIN PRESENTS.

We are its editors and authors
and biggest fans—and we'd
love to hear from YOU!

Subscribe today to our online blog at
www.iheartpresents.com

REQUEST YOUR FREE BOOKS!

2 FREE NOVELS PLUS 2
FREE GIFTS!

PASSION GUARANTEED SEDUCTION

YES! Please send me 2 FREE Harlequin Presents® novels and my 2 FREE gifts (gifts are worth about $10). After receiving them, if I don't wish to receive any more books, I can return the shipping statement marked "cancel." If I don't cancel, I will receive 6 brand-new novels every month and be billed just $4.05 per book in the U.S. or $4.74 per book in Canada, plus 25¢ shipping and handling per book and applicable taxes, if any*. That's a savings of close to 15% off the cover price! I understand that accepting the 2 free books and gifts places me under no obligation to buy anything. I can always return a shipment and cancel at any time. Even if I never buy another book, the two free books and gifts are mine to keep forever.

106 HDN ERRW 306 HDN ERRL

Name _____ (PLEASE PRINT)

Address _____ Apt. #

City _____ State/Prov. _____ Zip/Postal Code

Signature (if under 18, a parent or guardian must sign)

Mail to the **Harlequin Reader Service:**
IN U.S.A.: P.O. Box 1867, Buffalo, NY 14240-1867
IN CANADA: P.O. Box 609, Fort Erie, Ontario L2A 5X3

⁻Not valid to current subscribers of Harlequin Presents books.

Want to try two free books from another line?
Call 1-800-873-8635 or visit www.morefreebooks.com.

* Terms and prices subject to change without notice. N.Y. residents add applicable sales tax. Canadian residents will be charged applicable provincial taxes and GST. This offer is limited to one order per household. All orders subject to approval. Credit or debit balances in a customer's account(s) may be offset by any other outstanding balance owed by or to the customer. Please allow 4 to 6 weeks for delivery. Offer available while quantities last.

Your Privacy: Harlequin Books is committed to protecting your privacy. Our Privacy Policy is available online at www.eHarlequin.com or upon request from the Reader Service. From time to time we make our lists of customers available to reputable third parties who may have a product or service of interest to you. If you would prefer we not share your name and address, please check here. ☐

HP08

Don't forget Harlequin Presents EXTRA
now brings you a powerful new collection
every month featuring four books!

Be sure not to miss any of the titles in

In the Greek Tycoon's Bed,

available May 13:

THE GREEK'S
FORBIDDEN BRIDE
by Cathy Williams

THE GREEK TYCOON'S
UNEXPECTED WIFE
by Annie West

THE GREEK TYCOON'S
VIRGIN MISTRESS
by Chantelle Shaw

THE GIANNAKIS BRIDE
by Catherine Spencer

EXTRA

TALL, DARK AND SEXY

The men who never fail—seduction included!

Brooding, successful and arrogant, these men
can sweep any female they desire off her feet.
But now there's only one woman they want—
and they'll use their wealth, power, charm and
irresistibly seductive ways to claim her!

**Don't miss any of the titles in this exciting
collection available June 10, 2008:**

#9 THE BILLIONAIRE'S VIRGIN BRIDE
by **HELEN BROOKS**

#10 HIS MISTRESS BY MARRIAGE
by **LEE WILKINSON**

#11 THE BRITISH BILLIONAIRE AFFAIR
by **SUSANNE JAMES**

#12 THE MILLIONAIRE'S MARRIAGE REVENGE
by **AMANDA BROWNING**

*Harlequin Presents EXTRA delivers a themed
collection every month featuring 4 new titles.*

www.eHarlequin.com   HPE0608